DISNEY BIG HERO 6

THE JUNIOR NOVELIZATION

ISBN 978-0-7364-3188-0

randomhousekids.com

Printed in the United States of America

10 9 8 7 6 5 4 3 2 1

BIG HERO 6

THE JUNIOR NOVELIZATION

Adapted by Irene Trimble

Random House 🏠 New York

ビッグ・ヒーロー6

Chapter 1

Not quite a big city, and not quite a small town, San Fransokyo had always been a mysterious mix of old and new. On foggy nights, the bright skyscraper lights and the neon of the modern city softened, giving the old Victorian pagodas and forgotten alleyways of the past an inviting glow.

One such night, a young teenage boy named Hiro Hamada was making his way down an old brick alley. He was looking for a place where grown men came to fight.

The boy felt a little nervous when he finally approached a rowdy crowd. Men were jammed around a fighting ring, chanting, "Ya-ma! Ya-ma!"

Mr. Yama, a large, sumo-sized man, strutted into the ring and held up his huge hands in victory. It had been a fight "to the death," and

Mr. Yama's tricked-out eighteen-inch robot—which had claws for one hand and a spinning saw wheel for the other—had just decapitated the competition. The remains of the defeated robot were unceremoniously tossed onto a pile of other dismembered opponents.

"Who's next?" Mr. Yama snarled, scanning the crowd. The spectators exchanged money and prepared to place their bets. "Who has the guts to step into the ring with Little Yama?" The crowd stared at the big man's fierce robot and shrank away. Some even hid their bots behind their backs.

Then a voice said, "Can I try?" The crowd parted and everyone stared at Hiro.

Yama's eyes narrowed. "What's your name, little boy?"

"It's Hiro. Hiro Hamada."

The four-hundred pound man folded his thick arms over his chest. "Go home, Zero. Bot-fighting isn't for little boys with toy robots. You have to pay to play."

"Is this enough?" Hiro asked, holding up a wad of bills. Yama smiled and placed Little Yama back in the ring.

Hiro held up a small, unimpressive twelve-inch robot. He tried to seem confident. He'd learned a long time ago that when you bot-fought in this part of town, you never let them see your fear.

Hiro put Megabot down into the ring. Immediately, the tiny robot toppled over. Yama couldn't hide his smirk as he sat on his mat. Hiro also sat down, his mat across the ring from Yama's. The bettors went crazy. Piles of cash grew higher and higher.

The referee stepped up and lowered an open umbrella between the two. "Two bots enter! One bot leaves!" she shouted. "Fighters ready? Fight!"

Little Yama quickly advanced on Megabot, towering over him. In seconds, he had sliced through Hiro's bot! The crowd cheered.

But without warning, Hiro's seemingly broken bot reassembled. "Megabot, destroy!" Hiro ordered.

Hiro's bot counterattacked with such deadly force, the fight was over in seconds. Little Yama was torn to pieces. Bits of him sparked and jumped all over the ring.

With the click of Hiro's remote control, Megabot gave a cute yet awkward bow. The whole audience was silent.

Mr. Yama was stunned. "But . . . wha—? How? This is not possible!"

Hiro smiled. "No one likes a sore loser, big guy. But everyone loves a winner!" He held up his bot, and the crowd chanted, "Hi-ro! Hi-ro! Hi-ro!"

"No!" Mr. Yama yelled, and the crowd became silent. "No one can beat Little Yama. You cheated, and I want to know how! Give me that bot." Several of Mr. Yama's large associates suddenly moved toward Hiro.

"I can see you're upset. Here's what I'm gonna do: I'll teach you everything I know about high-torque micromotors," Hiro said as the huge men backed him into a corner. "I charge an hourly rate—it's pricey, but worth it. Before you know it, you'll be making robots that aren't totally junky. First class is free!" Hiro was really starting to sweat when a scooter came out of nowhere and tore down the alley. It skidded to a stop, knocking Mr. Yama and his goons to the ground.

"Get on!" the rider yelled to Hiro.

Chapter 2

Tadashi Hamada reached back and shoved a helmet on his little brother Hiro's head. He gunned the scooter's engine and took off through the crowd.

It was hard for Tadashi to be patient with his little brother sometimes. He turned and smacked the top of Hiro's helmet. "You graduated high school when you were thirteen, and this is what you're doing? You're wasting that big brain of yours!"

It was well known that both the Hamada brothers were tech prodigies, but Hiro—he was something special. He was a bona fide genius. Not that he did much with his brain other than build fighting bots.

"I'm on a roll, big brother," Hiro replied, grinning. "There's no stopping me now."

Just then, a police car with its red lights flashing pulled up and blocked the end of the alley.

"Oh, no," Tadashi groaned, realizing they'd been caught up in a gambling raid. It wasn't long before he and Hiro were headed to jail, along with Yama and everyone else the cops were able to catch.

A short time later, Tadashi sat in his cell, staring across the hall at Hiro. Because of Hiro's age, he was given his own cell, while Tadashi was locked up with Yama and his goons. Hiro could see that Tadashi was furious.

Finally, a police officer yelled, "Tadashi and Hiro Hamada!" The boys stepped out of their cells and glanced sheepishly at their aunt Cass. She'd come to pick them up, and she looked worried.

"Uh, hi, Aunt Cass," Tadashi said.

She rushed to embrace them both. "Are you guys okay? Tell me you're okay!"

"We're okay," Hiro said, ducking his head.

She twisted both their ears. "Then what were you two knuckleheads thinking?"

It was a long ride home. Aunt Cass started in on them as soon as she got behind the wheel. "For ten years, I've done the best I could to raise you. Have I been perfect? No."

Hiro and Tadashi nodded. They had expected

her to lecture them, and they knew they deserved it. They hated making her upset.

"Is it like the blind raising the blind? Yes," she continued as she parked her pickup in front of the café she owned, the Lucky Cat. It was on the first floor of an old Victorian, and they all lived together in the apartment upstairs.

"We're sorry," Tadashi said as they got out of the truck.

Hiro knew he had to say something, too. "We love you, Aunt Cass."

Hiro and Tadashi cringed at the CLOSED sign hanging in the window. They knew she'd had to close up to get them out of jail.

"Well, I love you, too!" she grumbled as they entered the café. She grabbed a giant pastry from the counter and took a bite. "Stress eating! Because of you," she mumbled with her mouth full. Then she walked upstairs to their apartment with her fat cat, Mochi, following her.

Hiro and Tadashi also went upstairs, to the bedroom they shared. Hiro gathered some tools that were scattered on his desk while Tadashi watched.

"I hope you've learned your lesson," Tadashi finally said.

"Absolutely," Hiro said.

"You've got your priorities straight?"

"I really do," Hiro replied, making an adjustment to his robot, then heading for the door.

"Wait. Where are you going?" Tadashi asked.

Hiro smiled. "There's another bot fight across town. If I book it, I can still get there on time."

Tadashi threw up his hands in frustration. "Seriously? Are you gonna keep hustling bot fights, or are you gonna do something with your life?"

Hiro fidgeted for a second. "What, like go to college like you so people can tell me stuff I already know?"

Tadashi shook his head. "Unbelievable. What would Mom and Dad say?"

Hiro shrugged. "They wouldn't say anything. They're gone."

The answer hurt. But it made Tadashi realize he was the only person who could steer Hiro in the right direction. "Fine," he said. "I'll take you."

"Really?" Hiro said, surprised.

"I can't stop you from going, but I'm not going to let you go on your own."

Tadashi rode off with his brother on the back of his scooter. But suddenly, he made a turn.

Chapter 3

Hiro looked around as Tadashi drove through the gates of the San Fransokyo Institute of Technology, often called SFIT for short. "What are we doing at your nerd school?" Hiro asked. "Bot fight's that way."

"Pit stop," Tadashi replied as he pulled up to a gleaming steel-and-glass building.

Hiro impatiently followed Tadashi into SFIT's robotics lab. "Is this gonna take long? Megabot wants to fight!"

"Relax, you big baby. We'll be in and out," Tadashi said as he led Hiro into the enormous lab.

"Oh, great. I get to see your lab," Hiro said sarcastically. Out of the corner of his eye, Tadashi saw Hiro's attitude change. His lab was high-tech heaven. Tadashi smiled.

"Heads up!" said a girl with purple-streaked

hair as she whizzed by on a bike. She stopped short and tossed the bike onto a rack. Tadashi walked over to her and smiled.

Hiro couldn't help himself. He had to touch the bike. "Whoa . . . electro-mag suspension," he said.

"Who are you?"

Hiro turned around to look at the girl. "Um, I'm . . . Tadashi's brother."

"Go Go, this is Hiro."

Go Go Tomago chewed her gum and nodded.

Hiro looked back at her bike. "Never seen electro-mag suspension on a bike before."

Go Go spun the bike's back wheel. In place of an axle, the wheel was suspended between two magnetic forks. The wheel seemed to float like magic between the magnetic frames.

"Zero resistance," Go Go told him. "Faster bike. But not fast enough." Then she took the wheel off and threw it in the trash. "Yet."

Hiro stared as she fired up a 3-D printer on the spot and began to create a new wheel. Then he heard a high-pitched hum coming from the other side of the lab. He saw a large, muscular guy with dreadlocks experimenting with lasers there. His work space was immaculately organized. Hiro headed for the machine.

"Whoa. Do not move. Behind the line, please."

Hiro stopped and looked down. He took one step back behind a white line that was taped on the floor.

"Hey, Wasabi," Tadashi said to him. "This is my brother, Hiro."

Wasabi, a physics student, nodded. "Hello, Hiro. Prepare to be amazed. Catch."

Wasabi tossed an apple up into the air, but when Hiro reached for it, the apple fell down in hundreds of wafer-thin pieces.

"Wow," Hiro said.

Wasabi grabbed a bottle and sprayed its contents into the air. Hundreds of green lasers were immediately visible. "There has never been an optic system so precise."

Hiro nodded, noticing that Wasabi carefully placed his spray bottle back into a particular circle on the table.

"I have a system. A place for everything; everything in its place," Wasabi said.

Just then, Go Go grabbed something from Wasabi's table. "Need this," she said as she whizzed past him.

"Hey, what are you …," Wasabi shouted, and went after her. "You're messing up my whole system!"

The boys were watching Wasabi chase Go Go when a sweet voice said, "Coming through."

Hiro and Tadashi turned to see Honey Lemon, a blond chemistry genius, rolling a large ball of metal across the floor. They stepped aside.

Tadashi smiled. "Honey, this is my little brother, Hiro."

Honey was thrilled. "Omigosh! Hi," she gushed. "Perfect timing! You're going to love this!" She pushed the ball onto a hydraulic lift. Then she dashed over to a large machine that held many chemical elements and used the touchscreen to select several of them.

"That's a whole lot of tungsten carbide . . . ," Hiro said.

"Four hundred pounds of it," Honey responded.

They watched as the machine combined the elements. Honey smiled and said, "Super-heat to eight hundred degrees, and voilà!"

The boys saw a stream of chemicals shoot out of the machine and spray the metal ball. Instantly, the entire orb was encased in a bright pink glow.

"Pretty great, huh?" Honey asked, and used her cell phone camera to snap a selfie of the boys and herself standing in front of the ball.

Hiro didn't know what to make of it. "So . . . pink," he said.

Honey nodded enthusiastically. Pink was her favorite color. "And here's the best part," she said.

With one touch, the metal ball disintegrated into dust.

"Wow!" Hiro said, stunned.

"I know, right?" Honey said. "I call it chemical-metal embrittlement."

"Not bad, Honey," Tadashi said with a smile.

Hiro thought Tadashi's friends were nice, but he was a little confused about their names. "Honey, Go Go, Wasabi . . . ?"

"I spill wasabi on my shirt one time, people—one time!" Wasabi said.

"Hey," Tadashi laughed, holding up his hands. "Talk to Fred. He gives out the nicknames."

"Who's Fred?" Hiro asked.

"This guy!" someone said behind Hiro. Turning, Hiro came face to face with a giant Japanese-style Kaiju monster—and screamed!

The monster took his big head off, and the smiling, friendly-looking kid underneath said, "Do not be alarmed. Name's Fred. School mascot by day." He spun the SFIT sign he was holding. "But by night, also school mascot."

Hiro nodded. "Hey. So what's your major?"

Fred plopped down on a couch strewn with comic books. "Oh, I'm not a student here," he said, grinning. "But I am a major science enthusiast! I've been trying to get Honey to develop a formula that can turn me into a fire-breathing lizard at will." Fred sighed. "But she says that's not science."

Honey nodded. "It's really not."

Fred called out to Wasabi, "Right. Then I guess the shrink ray I asked Wasabi for isn't science either, is it?"

Wasabi shook his head.

"Laser eyes? Tingly fingers?" Fred asked, following him.

Tadashi smiled and led Hiro to another part of the lab. "What have you been working on?" Hiro asked his brother.

"I'll show you."

Chapter 4

Tadashi took Hiro to his workstation. He rooted through a drawer and held up a roll of duct tape.

Hiro sighed. "Hate to break it to you, bro—already been invented."

Suddenly, Tadashi slapped a piece of the tape on Hiro's arm. "Hey! What's your deal?" Hiro asked.

Tadashi pointed to a small red suitcase on the ground and yanked the tape off Hiro's arm. "Owwww!" Hiro yelled.

A loud BEEP filled the room. The suitcase began to hum, and lights on it blinked to life. The top opened and a white vinyl form began to rise. When it was fully inflated, a huge, puffy figure stepped out of the suitcase

"Hello, I am Baymax, your personal health-care companion," it said.

"This is what I've been working on," Tadashi

said, gesturing at the robot.

Baymax turned to Hiro. "I was alerted to the need for medical attention when you said 'Ow.' What seems to be the trouble?"

Hiro rubbed his arm and snapped, "Sibling abuse."

"I will scan you now," Baymax said. "Scan complete. You have a small epidermal abrasion on your forearm."

"You've done some serious coding on this thing, huh?" Hiro asked Tadashi. Even though Hiro was still annoyed at his brother, he was also impressed.

Tadashi walked over to Baymax and removed a chip from his access port. "I programmed him with more than ten thousand medical procedures and a caregiving interface that makes Baymax . . . Baymax."

"I suggest an antibacterial spray," Baymax stated.

Tadashi slid the chip back in. Hiro was impressed. "Vinyl?" he asked.

Tadashi smiled. "I was going for a nonthreatening, huggable kind of thing."

"Looks like a walking marshmallow." Hiro said, turning to Baymax. "No offense."

"I am a robot," Baymax said as Hiro poked and

prodded him. "I cannot be offended."

Hiro waved his hands in front of Baymax's eyes. "Hyperspectral cameras?" he asked before pushing his face into Baymax's stomach. "Titanium skeleton?"

"Carbon-fiber," Tadashi responded. "He can lift five hundred pounds. He's gonna help a lot of people."

Baymax sprayed Hiro's arm with a disinfectant, then handed him a lollipop. Hiro tasted it and said, "Sugar-free? Bleh."

"I cannot deactivate until you say you are satisfied with your care."

"Well, then I am satisfied with my care," Hiro said. As Baymax deflated and folded neatly back into his red suitcase, a distinguished-looking man with graying hair approached them. It was Professor Callaghan.

"Burning the midnight oil, Mr. Hamada?" the professor asked. Then he looked at Hiro. "You must be Tadashi's brother. I've heard a lot about you. Bot-fighter, right?"

Hiro took his bot out of his pocket and fiddled with it.

Professor Callaghan reached for the bot, asking, "May I?"

Hiro handed it over, and Professor Callaghan

studied it for a moment, then smiled. "Magnetic-bearing servos—"

"Pretty sick, huh?" Hiro interrupted. "Want to see how I put them together?"

"Hey, genius," Tadashi said. "He invented them."

Hiro's eyes widened and his jaw dropped. "You invented . . . You're Robert Callaghan? Like, as in Callaghan's Law of Robotics?"

Professor Callaghan smiled. "That's right." He handed Hiro back his robot. "Have you ever thought about applying here?"

Tadashi said quickly, "Oh, I don't know. He's pretty serious about his career in bot-fighting."

Hiro shrugged. "Well, kind of serious."

"I can see why. With your bot, winning must come easy. And if you like things easy, my program isn't for you. We push the boundaries of robotics here." The professor put a hand on Tadashi's shoulder. "My students go on to shape the future."

Tadashi began to steer Hiro out the door. "Nice to meet you, Hiro," Callaghan called to him. "Good luck with the bot fights."

Hiro's mind was racing. He wanted to stay and push the boundaries of robotics, too. When they were outside, Tadashi revved up the scooter.

"You getting on?" Tadashi asked.

Hiro started pacing back and forth. "If I don't go to this nerd school, I'm going to lose my mind. How do I get in?" he asked. Tadashi smiled, happy that Hiro wanted to attend San Fransokyo Tech. Tadashi's not-so-subtle plan had worked.

Chapter 5

Tadashi came home the next day and stapled an SFIT poster over one of Hiro's bot-fighting posters. It announced SFIT's annual Tech Showcase—those entrants with the best tech would win admission to the school.

Hiro read it and looked at Tadashi in disbelief.

"You come up with something that blows Callaghan away and you're in," Tadashi said. "But it's gotta be great."

Hiro stared at the poster, smiling. "Trust me, it will be," he said, knowing this was his big chance. He rolled his chair to his desk and confidently set about designing the most awesome tech project SFIT had ever seen.

Hours later, all he had to show for his time were crumpled pieces of paper scattered all over the room. "Nothing. No ideas. Useless, empty brain,"

Hiro said as he banged his head against the top of his desk.

Tadashi looked over from where he was sitting on his bed. "Wow. Washed up at fourteen. So sad."

"I got nothing," Hiro complained. "I'm done. Dead end. I'm never getting it."

Tadashi went over and picked Hiro up, flipped him over, and held him upside down by his ankles. Hiro screamed.

"Shake things up!" Tadashi said. "Use that big brain of yours to think your way out."

"What?"

"There are no dead ends, Hiro," Tadashi told him.

Hanging upside down, Hiro noticed his battle bot on the floor. Suddenly, what he needed to do became crystal clear. He reached over and grabbed his bot, and when Tadashi let him down, he bolted out to the garage.

In the past, Hiro had used the garage as a lab for building his battle bots. It had everything he needed to create his new vision: multiple computer terminals, 3-D printers, the works. Hiro sat down, cracked his knuckles, and got to work.

Months passed. Hiro worked day and night. Aunt Cass checked on him and made sure he was fed.

Even Tadashi's friends from SFIT peeked in to see what this obsessed kid was doing. But Tadashi knew that whatever his brother was inventing would be great! Finally, the day of the showcase arrived.

The showcase hall at SFIT was jammed with judges, presenters, and several tech-industry representatives searching for new talent. All around the hall, kids held unrecognizable glass, steel, and plastic objects. They fidgeted with their projects and made last-minute adjustments.

"How you feeling?" Tadashi asked Hiro.

"Hey, you're talking to an ex-bot-fighter," Hiro said, jabbing at the air with his fist. "Takes a lot more than this to rattle me."

"Yup, he's nervous," Go Go said decisively.

Wasabi nodded. "What do you need, Hiro? Deodorant? Breath mint? Fresh pair of underpants? I come prepared."

"Guys, really. I'm chill," Hiro said.

Honey gave him a warm smile. "Relax," she said. "Your tech is amazing. Tell him, Go Go."

Go Go looked at Hiro. "Stop whining. Woman up."

Fred laughed and pointed to his chest. "Worry not, little fellow. Freddie wore his lucky Megazon shirt! Worn by the creator of Megazon himself."

Wasabi frowned. "Smells terrible."

"I know, right?" said Fred. "The creator died in this shirt. . . . Adds to the value."

Wasabi nearly gagged at the thought.

A spotlight hit the stage. The announcer said, "Next presenter, Hiro Hamada."

"Oh, you're on! Everybody say 'Hiro!'" Honey said as she took another selfie with Hiro and the gang.

"Do good science!" Fred cheered as he walked off with the rest of their friends. They wanted spots in the front row of the audience for Hiro's presentation.

Alone with his brother, Tadashi noticed that Hiro's confidence seemed to have vanished. "Hey, what's going on, huh? What happened to Mr. Battle Bot?"

Hiro had a worried look in his eyes. "I really want to go here."

"Just take a breath—you got this," Tadashi said with a squeeze of Hiro's shoulder.

Hiro followed his brother's advice, smiled, and walked onto the stage.

ビッグ・ヒーロー6

Chapter 6

Hiro walked up to the mike. He looked out at the huge crowd . . . and felt a heaviness in the pit of his stomach. They were all staring at him, waiting.

"Uh, hi," Hiro said into the mike, which screeched with feedback. For a moment, his mind went blank. Then he saw Tadashi's face in the audience as his brother moved to stand next to Aunt Cass. He was smiling and giving Hiro a thumbs-up.

Hiro smiled back and took a breath. "Sorry. My name is Hiro Hamada, and I've been working on something I think is pretty cool. I hope you like it."

Hiro put on a headset and reached into his hoodie. He took out a small object no bigger than a paper clip. "This is a microbot." The small object in his palm took a bow. "It doesn't look like much," Hiro continued, "but when it links up with the rest of its pals, things get a little more interesting."

The crowd didn't seem impressed. Then a murmur rose as the startled audience noticed waves of tiny microbots slithering across the floor. The single microbot flew from Hiro's hand and joined a towering column of microbots that had now formed onstage.

Hiro smiled and tapped his headset. "The microbots are controlled with this neural transmitter." He took the headset off and the microbots collapsed to the floor. They re-formed into a column as soon as Hiro put the headset back on.

"I think of what I want them to do," Hiro said, "and they do it!" The microbots took the shape of a hand waving. Everyone in the audience smiled and waved back. "The applications for this tech are limitless. Take construction."

Hiro stared at the microbots, and with a wave of his hand, they picked up cinder blocks and assembled them into a tower. "What used to take teams of people working by hand for months or years can now be accomplished by one person!"

Then the microbots lifted Hiro and placed him on top of the tower. In the audience, billionaire tech mogul Alistair Krei was very impressed.

"And that's just the beginning," Hiro said as he

leaped off the tower. Everyone gasped, thinking he was about to fall, but the microbots rose and caught him midair. Hiro smiled. He could see Tadashi giving him another thumbs-up.

"How about transportation?" Hiro asked. The microbots transformed into a set of legs that walked Hiro through the audience. "Microbots can move anything, anywhere, with ease."

As they approached the stage, the microbots formed a set of stairs so Hiro could climb back up to it. "If you can think it, the microbots can do it!" Hiro said.

The audience was with him now. The moment belonged to Hiro, and he was on a roll. "The only limit is your imagination! Microbots!" he exclaimed, and the audience burst into applause.

Hiro jumped off the stage and found Tadashi. The two high-fived as Aunt Cass shouted enthusiastically, "That's my nephew! Whoo! My family! I love my family!"

Chapter 7

The showcase hall was buzzing as students waited for the judges' results. Hiro, Tadashi, and the gang were anxiously waiting, too, when a large, imposing figure approached them. It was Alistair Krei.

"That was an impressive display," Krei said, gesturing to Hiro's microbot. "May I?" He took the microbot from Hiro and turned it in his fingers. "With some development, these could be revolutionary. That's why I want them at Krei Tech."

"Shut up!" Hiro exclaimed in disbelief.

Krei smiled. "You're about to become a very wealthy kid."

"Shut up!" Hiro repeated.

But Hiro and his friends weren't the only ones who heard Krei's offer. Professor Callaghan did, too. "Hiro," he said, "Mr. Krei is right. Your microbots are an inspired piece of tech. You can continue to develop them. Or you can sell them to a man who is only guided by his own self-interest."

Krei held up a hand. "Robert, I know how you feel about me, but it shouldn't affect this young man's opportunity to—"

Professor Callaghan cut him off. "This is your decision, Hiro. But you should know, Mr. Krei has cut corners and ignored sound science to get where he is."

"That's just not true," Krei argued.

"I wouldn't trust Krei Tech with your microbots," Callaghan said, staring straight at Krei. "Or anything else."

Everyone was surprised by the professor's statement. They looked at Hiro, waiting for an answer.

"Hiro, I'm offering you more money than a fourteen-year-old could imagine," Krei said.

Hiro looked at Tadashi, but his brother smiled at him, knowing he would make the right decision. "I appreciate the offer, Mr. Krei. But they're not for sale."

Krei seemed surprised and a bit insulted. It wasn't often that he heard the word "no," and he didn't like it. "I thought you were smarter than that," Krei said to Hiro. But Hiro's face was unchanged.

Once Krei realized there wasn't going to be a sale, he spun on his heel. "Robert," he said, addressing Callaghan as he started to leave.

But Tadashi stopped him. "Mr. Krei?" he said, tapping him on the shoulder.

Krei turned and Tadashi pointed to the large man's hand. "That's my brother's."

Krei opened his hand and seemed surprised that he'd somehow walked off with Hiro's microbot. "Oh, that's right," he said with a chuckle. But Tadashi knew better. Krei tossed the microbot to Hiro, who stuffed it back in his pocket.

"You made the right choice," Callaghan said, and handed Hiro an envelope with the SFIT crest on it. "I look forward to seeing you in class."

Hiro beamed. He did it. He had won admittance to SFIT!

Hiro and the gang burst from the showcase hall. Aunt Cass pulled them into a group hug. "All right, geniuses, let's feed those hungry brains," she said. "Back to the café! Dinner is on me!"

Fred was the most excited. "Yes!" he shouted. "Nothing is better than free food!"

Tadashi smiled. It had been a perfect day. "Aunt Cass? We'll catch up, okay?"

"Sure. I'm so proud of you. I'm proud of you both," she replied, hugging Tadashi and Hiro again.

"Hey, where are you going?" Hiro asked Tadashi as Aunt Cass and their friends headed for the Lucky Cat. Hiro thought maybe Tadashi wanted to help him gather up his microbots in the showcase hall. But Tadashi threw his arm around his brother and the two walked onto the campus.

Minutes later, Hiro and Tadashi were staring at the gleaming steel-and-glass robotics building in the distance.

"I know what you're going to say," Hiro said. "I should be proud of myself because I'm using my 'gift' for something important."

"No," Tadashi replied. "I was just gonna tell you your fly was down through the whole showcase."

Hiro looked panicked as Tadashi laughed. Then Hiro slugged him in the arm for making him look. "Ha-ha. Hilarious," Hiro said.

But Hiro became serious. "Hey. I wouldn't be here if it wasn't for you. So . . . thanks."

"You don't have to say that. I mean, it's true,

but you don't have to say it," Tadashi said.

The two brothers threw fake punches and began to wrestle as they laughed.

When they turned back to go collect Hiro's microbots, they were surprised to see black smoke billowing from the showcase hall. It seemed impossible, but the hall was on fire!

As Hiro and Tadashi ran toward the burning building, they saw people running out, gasping and coughing. The entrance was nearly engulfed in flames.

Tadashi stopped and grabbed a student. "Are you okay?" he asked.

"Yeah, I'm fine. Callaghan's still in there!"

Tadashi began to run toward the entrance. Hiro knew his brother was going to try to save the professor.

"Tadashi, no!" Hiro said, grabbing his shirt.

"Callaghan is still in there," Tadashi said. "Someone has to help!"

Hiro reluctantly let go of his brother and watched helplessly as Tadashi ran into the showcase hall.

Inside was an inferno. But through the heat and smoke, Tadashi saw Professor Callaghan. Before Tadashi could reach him, he heard a large beam crack above his head.

Outside, Hiro heard a deafening boom and was knocked to the ground as the hall exploded.

"Tadashi!" Hiro yelled. He saw Tadashi's baseball cap lying on the ground nearby. He picked it up and cried, "Tadashi! Tadashi!"

Chapter 8

The next day, a makeshift memorial had been arranged at the entrance to the university. Students had placed flowers and candles near pictures of Tadashi and Professor Callaghan.

Friends gathered at the Lucky Cat Café to grieve and support each other, but Hiro sat on the stairs, away from everyone else. None of it consoled him.

For weeks, Hiro barely left his room. He sat in his beanbag chair and numbly played with his old battle bot. The blinds were closed and plates of food were usually left untouched.

One morning, Aunt Cass softly knocked on Hiro's door. "Hey, sweetie," she said, coming in. "I brought you some breakfast. You get any sleep?" Then she noticed that Hiro's bed was still perfectly made.

"Yeah, sure," Hiro replied.

Aunt Cass opened the blinds to let in some light. "Hey, Mrs. Matsuda's in the café. She's wearing something super inappropriate for an eighty-year-old. That always cracks you up. You should come down."

"Maybe later," Hiro said.

Aunt Cass nodded. "Okay," she said. "No rush. Come down whenever." Then she added, "The university called again. It's been a few weeks since classes started, but they said it's not too late to register."

"Okay. Thanks," Hiro said. "I'll think about it."

When Aunt Cass left, Hiro got up and closed the blinds again. Out of the corner of his eye, he noticed an icon on his computer screen blinking at him. A video of his friends popped open. Go Go, Honey, Fred, and Wasabi stared back at him.

"Hey, Hiro!" they called in unison.

"We just wanted to check in and see how you are doing," Honey said.

Wasabi smiled. "Wish you were here, buddy."

"We should hang out soon, okay . . . ," Fred piped up.

Hiro hit a button, and silence filled the room. He sighed as his eyes moved across his desk, stopping as they fell on a letter from SFIT. Anger and despair filled him, and he grabbed the letter and tossed it in the trash. He picked up Megabot, his fighting bot, and the bottom of it fell off, landing on his foot. "Ow!" he yelled.

Hiro hopped up and down for a minute, and then he saw something moving on Tadashi's side of the room. He was stunned for a moment. He stared as a white shape rose and began to take form. It was Baymax!

Once Baymax had fully inflated, he shuffled and shimmied his enormous white body to Hiro's side of the room. His big belly and behind knocked over books and lamps along the way. "Hello," he said finally. "I am Baymax, your personal health-care companion."

Hiro had forgotten all about Tadashi's last project. "Hey, Baymax," he said. "I didn't know you were still ... active."

"I heard a sound of distress. What seems to be the trouble?"

Hiro wiggled the toes of his hurt foot. "Oh, I just stubbed my toe a little. I'm fine."

Icons with smiling and scowling faces representing degrees of pain appeared on Baymax's chest. "On a scale of one to ten, how would you rate your pain?" he said.

"Zero," Hiro replied, flicking his hands, trying to

shoo the robot away. "I'm okay, really. You can . . . uh, shrink now."

Baymax reached down with a big puffy arm and waddled forward. "Does it hurt when I touch it?"

Hiro backed up. "What are you doing? No. No touching. I'm fine."

Hiro tripped on the rug and fell, wedging himself between his bed and dresser. Baymax loomed over him. "You have fallen," he said.

Hiro rolled his eyes. "You think?" he asked, grabbing a shelf above his dresser to pull himself up. The shelf tipped and Hiro's toys and speakers slid off. "Ow!" Hiro yelled as first a book and then a large robot toy hit him on the head.

"On a scale of—" Baymax kept saying as more items hit Hiro on the head.

"Ow!" Hiro shouted as the last thing fell.

"On a scale of one to ten, how would you rate your pain?" Baymax asked.

Hiro rubbed his head, clearly in pain, and said, "Zero!"

Baymax reached down and picked Hiro up. Alarmed, Hiro tried to push the big arms away.

"It is all right to cry," Baymax said. "Crying is a natural response to pain. I will scan your injuries."

"I'm not crying!" Hiro shouted, struggling out

of Baymax's embrace. Hiro quickly backed away. "And you don't need to scan me!"

"Scan complete," Baymax said in a flash.

"Unbelievable," Hiro grumbled.

"You have sustained no injuries. However, your hormone and neurotransmitter levels indicate you are experiencing mood swings, common in adolescence. Diagnosis: puberty."

"Whoa! Okay!" Hiro said, grabbing for Baymax's suitcase. "Time to shrink now."

"You should expect an increase in body hair, especially in your armpits and on your legs, chest, and—"

"Thank you! That's enough!" Hiro said, pushing Baymax toward his charging station. "Let's get you back to your luggage."

"I cannot deactivate until you say you are satisfied with my care."

"Fine," Hiro said. "I'm satisfied with my—"

But before Hiro could finish, he tripped over Baymax's foot and landed flat on the floor.

As he lay there, he noticed a hoodie under his bed. It was the one he had worn to the SFIT Showcase. The hoodie was moving softly, causing dust to rise in little puffs. Then it started to vibrate and shake!

ビッグ・ヒーロー6

Chapter 9

Hiro pulled the hoodie out from under his bed. He sat up and quickly searched the pockets. "My microbot!" he said, pulling one out. It was the bot he'd used in his demonstration, and somehow, it was still vibrating. "This doesn't make sense."

"Puberty can often be a confusing time for a young adolescent flowering into manhood."

"No," Hiro replied. He put the microbot into a glass petri dish and placed a lid on top. The small bot continued to vibrate. "This thing's attracted to the other microbots," he said to himself. "But they were all destroyed in the fire. Dumb thing must be broken."

He tossed the petri dish on his desk and grabbed Megabot, turning his back on Baymax and the microbot.

Baymax looked down at the petri dish. The

microbot kept banging against one side of the glass.

Baymax said, "Your tiny robot is trying to go somewhere."

Exasperated, Hiro stared up at the ceiling. "Oh, yeah? Why don't you find out where it's trying to go."

Baymax nodded and picked up the petri dish. "Would it stabilize your pubescent mood swings?"

"Uh-hmm, absolutely," Hiro said, hoping Baymax would finally leave him in peace.

Hiro expected Baymax to ponder the problem. Instead he headed out the door! Before Hiro knew it, the big robot was gone!

Hearing cars honking outside, Hiro looked out the window and saw Baymax heading into traffic, cars screeching to avoid hitting him. He threw on his hoodie and dashed out of his room. He was halfway down the stairs when Aunt Cass saw him.

"Hiro!" she said. "You're up and dressed. That's great! Are you registering for school?"

Hiro skidded to a stop and tried to sound casual. "Uh, yeah. That's it. Exactly. Registering for classes."

"Are you sure you're ready?" Aunt Cass asked.

Hiro heard the sound of more horns honking outside. "So ready," Hiro replied.

"Okay, special dinner tonight! I'll whip up some chicken wings, you know, with the hot sauce that makes our faces numb?"

Hiro nodded quickly. "Sounds good," he said. He was about to run off when Aunt Cass gave him a big hug. Hiro hugged her back, then dodged out the door.

He ran down the street, but there was no sign of Baymax anywhere. He followed the sound of cars hitting the brakes and tires screeching until he finally got a glimpse of the big white robot. He was on the back of a cable car.

"Baymax!" Hiro yelled.

ビッグ・ヒーロー6

Chapter 10

Hiro chased the cable car as it headed downhill. "Hey! Hold up! Stop!" he yelled. But by the time Hiro reached it, Baymax had hopped off.

Hiro glanced in stores and down streets. He searched everywhere before finally looking up. A puffy white figure strolled along the edge of the elevated train tracks. Hiro gasped as a train rushed past and almost knocked the robot off of the ledge. "Baymax!" he shouted, but he had lost him again.

He continued to follow the sounds of traffic chaos, knowing it was probably Baymax who was causing the commotion.

Hiro was almost out of breath. He stopped and took a look around. He'd been too focused on Baymax to notice, but now he realized he was in a run-down, industrial part of town. Everything looked dark and abandoned.

Then he saw Baymax! He was standing outside a grimy old warehouse.

"Baymax!" Hiro shouted. "Are you crazy? What are you doing?"

Baymax held up the glass petri dish. "I have found out where your tiny robot wants to go."

Hiro looked at the petri dish. The microbot was really banging against the dish in the direction of the warehouse. Hiro had thought the microbot was malfunctioning, but now he had to consider the possibility that maybe it wasn't.

Even so, how could he get into the warehouse? He ran to a metal door and pulled on it, but just as he had expected, it was locked.

"There's a window," Baymax said, pointing to an upper story.

Moments later, Hiro was standing on Baymax's giant head. "Please exercise caution," Baymax warned as Hiro partially deflated the robot's head with the weight of his feet. "A fall from this height could lead to bodily harm."

Hiro climbed through the window and into the warehouse. In the dim light, all he could see were oil drums on a lower level.

"Oh, no."

At Baymax's declaration, Hiro looked back. He

saw that the robot had gotten stuck trying to get through the window.

Baymax suddenly made a rude noise. "Excuse me," the robot said, "while I let out some air."

"Uh, okay." Hiro understood that to fit through the window, Baymax had to deflate a bit, but the sound was really obnoxious—and loud. "Are you done?" Hiro whispered.

"Yes," Baymax replied, and Hiro pulled him through. "It will take me a moment to reinflate."

"Fine," Hiro said, rolling his eyes. "Just keep it down."

Leaving Baymax behind to inflate, Hiro nervously went down a flight of creaky stairs. As he passed a row of oil drums, he thought he heard a low drone. "Hello?" he asked, but no one answered. He grabbed a broom.

Hiro turned a corner and saw a sealed-off area in the middle of the warehouse, covered with tarps. He crept closer and peeked inside. He was shocked to see a large machine manufacturing . . . Could it be? . . . Yes! Microbots! Lots of them. They were being spit out by the machine onto a conveyer belt.

"My microbots?" Hiro whispered. "Someone's making more."

"Hiro," a voice suddenly said.

"GAH!" Hiro gasped and turned around. It was only Baymax. "You gave me a heart attack!"

Baymax nodded and waddled closer. "My hands are equipped with defibrillators. Clear," he said as he rubbed his hands together and held them up to Hiro's chest, ready to shock his heart into a normal rhythm.

"Stop! It's just an expression!" Hiro said, and he walked over to one of the oil drums. He opened the lid and looked inside. It was filled with microbots. He looked up and down the aisle and realized that all the drums in the huge warehouse were filled with microbots!

Suddenly, the microbot in Hiro's petri dish started to shake, this time banging the petri dish on all sides.

"Oh, no," Baymax said again as a low, angry buzz rose from the oil drums all around them. The thousands of microbots rose out of the drums in a menacing swarm and headed toward Hiro and Baymax.

Hiro gave Baymax a look of terror and yelled, "Run!"

◀ Chapter 11 ▶

Hiro dashed for the warehouse door, clutching the petri dish. He didn't know who was controlling the microbots, but he knew they were behaving more like deadly insects than bots that were created to benefit mankind. Hiro looked over his shoulder and saw Baymax slowly waddling behind him. A wave of microbots was right on his tail. "Oh, come on!" Hiro yelled.

"I am not fast," Baymax said.

"Yeah, no kidding," Hiro said as he ran back and grabbed Baymax by the arm. "Go! Go!" Hiro told him until they had finally reached the door. Hiro pulled on it, then remembered it was locked. "Come on, kick it down!" he said to Baymax. "Punch it!"

In what seemed like slow motion, Baymax kicked the door. It was like a balloon hitting a brick wall. Hiro hung his head. But there was no time to mope. He jumped into some service tunnels under the floor and pulled Baymax in after him.

"Come on! Come on!" Hiro said, leading Baymax up the service tunnels to the second floor. They jumped out and headed for the window they had come in through. But again, Baymax got stuck.

Exasperated, Hiro looked back and saw a tall, dark figure in a white-and-red Kabuki mask. He was lurking in the shadows. It was impossible, but he seemed to be directing the microbots. The masked man must somehow have a neural transmitter as well!

Hiro was desperate now. He tried to shove Baymax through the window, yelling, "Come on! Suck it in!" But Baymax only flipped over, leaving Hiro dangling outside.

Suddenly, the microbots hit Baymax's face and upper body, riddling him with tiny holes. Like a punctured balloon, Baymax began to deflate, and the force of the escaping air jetted him and Hiro toward the ground with a whoosh!

Baymax cradled Hiro as they fell, his body absorbing the blow when they hit the pavement. They scrambled to their feet. "Come on! Let's get out of here! Go! Hurry!"

They ran for their lives. To Hiro's relief, he saw the lights of a police station up ahead. "Go this way!" he yelled to Baymax.

Hiro dragged Baymax inside the station and caught his breath. He gathered his thoughts and walked over to a policeman behind a desk. After twenty minutes of conversation with the sergeant, the officer said, "All right, let me get this straight: a man with a Kabuki mask attacked you with an army of miniature flying robots?"

"Microbots," Hiro replied, nodding. "He was controlling them telepathically with a neurocranial transmitter."

The officer scratched his head. "So Mr. Kabuki was using ESP to attack you and balloon man over here?"

"He's a robot," Hiro said as Baymax reached for a piece of tape from the dispenser on the officer's desk. The robot's internal motors tried to re-inflate him, but the microbots had punched too many holes in his vinyl skin. The air coming out the holes made a high, squeaky sound. Baymax covered one hole with the tape and started the process over again.

"Did you file a report when your flying robots were stolen?" the officer asked, moving the tape dispenser closer to Baymax. The noises coming from Baymax changed pitch with every hole he patched.

"No!" Hiro replied. "I thought they were all destroyed. Look, I know it sounds nuts, but Baymax was there, too." He turned to Baymax and said, "Tell him!"

"Yes, Officer, it's truuuuuue." Baymax was suddenly slurring his words.

"What the—?" Hiro said, looking at Baymax. "What's wrong with you?"

"Loooowww ... baaatterryy ...," Baymax replied. Hiro looked at him closely and saw that the robot's eye lenses were having difficulty focusing. Baymax was starting to sway.

Hiro took hold of his arm and tried to steady him. "Whoa, whoa, whoa. Try to keep it together."

"I'm health care!" Baymax shouted. "Your personal Baymax companion!"

The sergeant had seen enough. "Kid," he said, "how about we call your parents and get them down here." He turned in his swivel chair and grabbed a notepad. "Just write your name and number down here...."

But by the time he turned around, Hiro and Baymax were gone. All that was left was a long piece of tape that stretched from the sergeant's desk to the precinct door.

‹ CHAPTER 12 ›

Outside, Hiro and Baymax were slowly making their way down the street. "I've got to get you home to your charging station," Hiro said. "Can you walk?"

Baymax took another step and plopped down on his butt. "I will scan you now," he slurred. "Scan complete. Health care!" Baymax shouted, waving a partially deflated arm.

"Sure, buddy. We're almost there," Hiro said, keeping the woozy robot moving. Finally, the Lucky Cat Café was in sight.

As Hiro struggled to get Baymax into the house, he said, "Okay, if my aunt asks, we were at school all day. Got it?"

"We jumped out a window," Baymax said.

"No!" Hiro responded. "Quiet! Shhh."

"Shhh. We jumped out a window," Baymax

repeated, his voice quieter as Hiro guided him up the stairs inside the house. But the robot missed a step and fell on his forehead with a thud.

"We can't say things like that around Aunt Cass!" Hiro reprimanded him.

Aunt Cass yelled, "Hiro? You home, sweetie?" She leaned over the kitchen counter. From her angle, she could only see Hiro's face at the top of the stairs.

Hiro froze. "Uh, that's right."

"I thought I heard you. Look at my little college man!" she said. "Oh, I can't wait to hear all about it! Oh, and wings are almost ready!" She returned to the stove, and Baymax stuck his head around the corner.

"Wiiiings!" Baymax said excitedly.

"Will you be quiet?" Hiro whispered, pushing him up the second set of stairs, toward his and Tadashi's room.

"Yeah! Wiiiings! Get ready to get your face melted!" Aunt Cass said. She placed a platter of red-hot chicken wings on the table. "Now, sit down and tell me everything!" But Hiro was already halfway to his room.

"Uh, the thing is," Hiro called to her, "since I registered so late, I've got a lot of school stuff to catch up on."

Aunt Cass heard a loud thump and looked toward Hiro's door. "What was that?" she asked.

"Mochi, that darn cat!" Hiro said, shaking his fist, hoping the cat wasn't in the kitchen.

Aunt Cass sighed. "Well, at least take a plate for the road, okay?"

Hiro dashed into the kitchen and grabbed a plate of wings. "Thanks for understanding," he told her, then rushed into his room and closed the door.

Baymax was sitting on the floor, cuddling the cat and mumbling, "Hairy baby, hairrry baby."

Hiro rolled his eyes and pushed Baymax over to his charger. He kept babbling, "Hello. I'm health care. Your personal Baymax companion."

"One foot in front of the other," Hiro guided him.

With Baymax in place, Hiro fell back onto his bed and finally took a breath.

He was so confused. What were all his microbots doing in a warehouse? And what was he supposed to do with this big white robot? "This doesn't make any sense," Hiro said.

As Baymax slowly powered back up, he could feel Hiro's distress. Baymax's blurry vision quickly snapped into focus. He scanned the room. Then, standing tall, he said, "Tadashi."

ビッグ・ヒーロー6

⟨ Chapter 13 ⟩

Hiro sat up like a shot. Baymax had definitely gotten his attention. "What?" Hiro asked. He saw Baymax holding Tadashi's baseball cap.

"Tadashi," Baymax repeated.

Hiro nodded and said, "Tadashi's gone."

"When will he return?" Baymax asked.

Hiro lowered his head and said, "He's dead, Baymax."

Baymax seemed confused. "Tadashi was in excellent health. With a proper diet and exercise, he should have lived a long life."

"Yeah," Hiro replied. "He should have. But there was a fire . . . and now he's gone."

Baymax pointed to his chest. "Tadashi is here—"

"No," Hiro cut him off. He pushed the robot's hand away. "People keep saying he's not really gone as long as we remember him. I don't buy it. It still hurts."

Baymax scanned Hiro. "I see no evidence of physical injury."

"It's a different kind of hurt," Hiro said, watching the robot step out of his charging platform.

"You are my patient. I would like to help," he stated.

Hiro shook his head. "You can't fix this one, buddy."

Baymax couldn't accept that answer. He was programmed to help his patient in any way possible. He turned to Hiro's computer and began to access information.

"Uh, what are you doing?" Hiro asked.

"I'm downloading a database on personal loss. Database downloaded. Treatments include contact with friends and loved ones. I am contacting them now."

"No, no, no . . . I, I . . . don't do that!" Hiro said, and shook his head. How could he explain to Baymax that he just didn't know how to be around people right now? He couldn't pretend things were okay, and he couldn't be sad around them, either.

"Your friends have been contacted," Baymax said.

"Unbelievable," Hiro grumbled, and Baymax

suddenly reached out and gave him a hug. "What are you doing?" Hiro asked.

"Other treatments include compassion and physical reassurance."

"I'm okay, really," Hiro said, trying to push him away. But then he realized Baymax was trying to help. Hiro gave him a hug back .

"You will be all right. There, there," Bamax said, patting Hiro on the back.

Hiro couldn't help but smile. "Thanks, Baymax." He had to admit, the hug did make him feel a little better.

"I am sorry about the fire," Baymax said.

"It's okay. It was an accident," Hiro replied. He had never talked about it before, but once he'd said "accident," the wheels in his mind started turning. He looked up at Baymax. "Unless … unless it wasn't."

Then all at once, the pieces fell together. "The guy in the mask stole my microbots, and then he set the fire to cover his tracks!" Hiro exclaimed. "We gotta catch that guy!"

Hiro was suddenly reenergized. He now had a purpose. He had to find the guy in the mask. But how? He'd already tried the police. They weren't going to help.

He put his hand on Baymax's arm, remembering

that in addition to being deflated, it was also covered in tape. The robot wasn't built for battle. But bot-fighting was a pastime Hiro was very familiar with. He suddenly saw Baymax as a giant version of one of his fighting bots. "But first, you're gonna need some upgrades."

Hiro's mind was racing with ideas as he snuck Baymax past Aunt Cass and out to the garage.

Chapter 14

Hiro couldn't wait to get started. He had Baymax stand in the center of the garage. "Okay, arms up," he said as he pulled an electronic device from a shelf. He quickly scanned Baymax, then rolled his chair over to his computer.

"Will apprehending the man in the mask improve your emotional state?" Baymax asked.

Hiro nodded. "Absolutely." Then he cracked his knuckles and turned his computer on. "All right. Let's work on your moves."

He downloaded the scanned image of Baymax to his computer. A 3-D model of Baymax's soft body appeared on the screen. With Baymax peering curiously over his shoulder, Hiro began to program a new fighting chip.

On another screen, Hiro downloaded a martial arts video. With a smile, he linked the karate moves to the model of Baymax. Once the program was running, Hiro turned his chair around and looked at the robot.

"Now let's take care of this," he said, poking at Baymax's vinyl belly. Hiro turned to a different computer screen and uploaded images of armor from throughout the ages. Hiro enjoyed mixing and matching the pieces until he came up with a suit of armor he liked.

He typed in the code that programmed his 3-D printer. With just a push of the print button, it created three-dimensional carbon-fiber objects in minutes. Hiro grabbed the first piece of armor and rolled his chair to where Baymax was waiting.

As he fitted each armor segment to Baymax, the fighting chip programming continued on another screen. The 3-D Baymax model was learning elaborate karate moves with every passing second.

Hiro finally added the last piece of armor to Baymax's soft body. "Now, that's more like it!" he said, admiring the hard shiny discs.

Hiro triumphantly placed a helmet on Baymax's head.

But Baymax simply stared at his armor. "I have some concerns," he said, tapping his hard belly.

"This armor may undermine my nonthreatening, huggable design."

Hiro couldn't help laughing. "That's kind of the idea, buddy. You look sick!"

"I cannot be sick. I am a robot," Baymax said.

Just then, an alert came from Hiro's computer: "Data transfer complete." The fighting program was ready! The red chip popped out of the drive and Hiro drew a skull on it.

He rolled over to Baymax and opened his access port. Then he gasped when he saw Baymax's green health-care chip—Tadashi's name was written on it. Hiro froze for a second. It hurt to see Tadashi's handwriting. But then he remembered why he was doing this, and slid the fighting chip in next to Tadashi's.

"I fail to see how karate makes me a better health-care companion," Baymax stated.

"You want to keep me healthy, don't you?" Hiro asked as he gathered a pile of wooden boards to test out the new programming. But Baymax still didn't understand. Finally, Hiro held a board in front of Baymax and said, "Punch this."

With almost no effort, Baymax snapped the board in two.

"Ha! Yes!" Hiro yelled. He held up a series of boards and gave Baymax new commands.

"Hammer fist!" Hiro said, and Baymax shattered the board.

"Knife hand!" Hiro ordered, and the edge of Baymax's hand hit the board like a guillotine.

"Back kick!" Hiro shouted, and with the grace of a ninja, the giant robot split the board with his foot, launching the pieces out the garage door.

Hiro continued to have Baymax practice karate moves. Baymax's work was flawless. Hiro smiled approvingly and held up his hand. "Yeah! Fist bump!"

Baymax stared at Hiro's hand and blinked. "Fist bump is not in my fighting database."

Hiro laughed. "No, this isn't a fighting thing. It's what people do when they're excited . . . you know, pumped up." Hiro bumped his fist against Baymax's and made an exploding sound.

Baymax blinked and made a mock exploding sound, too: "Bata-lata-la."

"There! Now you're getting it!" Hiro said.

Baymax nodded. "I will add fist bump to my caregiving matrix."

Hiro kicked the garage door open and stepped out with a fully armored Baymax. "All right," he said. "Now let's go get that guy!"

ビッグ・ヒーロー6

Hiro led Baymax back to the old warehouse that had been filled with barrels of microbots, never noticing that a car was following them every step of the way.

He walked up to the warehouse door, but this time it didn't matter whether it was locked. He pointed to the door and Baymax smashed it.

Hiro peeked into the dark warehouse carefully from behind his robot and said, "Get him, Baymax!"

But the warehouse was empty. Hiro was puzzled. "We're too late," he said. He took the petri dish out of his hoodie and watched it. The microbot was vibrating very softly in one direction.

"Your tiny robot is trying to go somewhere," Baymax said.

Hiro turned and walked in the direction the

HIRO HAMADA

The Brain

Abilities

* Genius-level brain power, allowing him to build, modify, and program nearly anything

Super Suit Features

* Integrated communications (helmet)
* Integrated computer, tracking, and programming interface (gloves/gauntlets)
* Industrial electromagnetic pads (gloves, knee pads, and shoes)

	AVERAGE		SUPER		EXCEPTIONAL		
Intelligence								GENIUS
Strength								
Durability								
Speed								
Energy						MAGNETIC		
Fighting								
Utility								

BAYMAX

The Guardian

ベイマックス

Abilities

* Advanced scanning optics
  (hyperspectral cameras for eyes)
* Programmed with over 10,000
  medical procedures
* Able to diagnose and treat patients
* Can fly with Hiro on his back

Super Suit Features

* Integrated communications (helmet)
* Rocket thrusters on feet for flight
* Rocket fists
* Armored body that increases strength

	AVERAGE	SUPER	EXCEPTIONAL	
Intelligence				
Strength				
Durability				ARMOR
Speed				FLYING
Energy		ELECTRIC		
Fighting				
Utility				

GO GO TOMAGO

The Speed

ゴーゴートマゴ

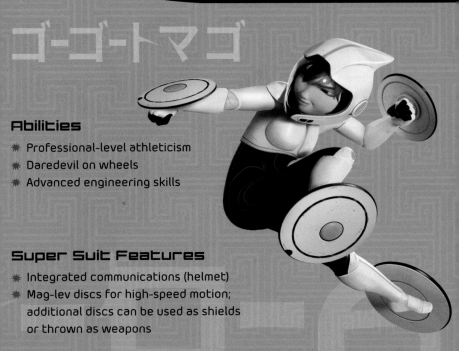

Abilities

* Professional-level athleticism
* Daredevil on wheels
* Advanced engineering skills

Super Suit Features

* Integrated communications (helmet)
* Mag-lev discs for high-speed motion; additional discs can be used as shields or thrown as weapons

	AVERAGE		SUPER		EXCEPTIONAL	
Intelligence						
Strength						
Durability						
Speed						WHEELS
Energy						
Fighting						DISCS
Utility						

HONEY LEMON

The Chemist

ハニーレモン

Abilities

* Brilliant chemist, able to create custom compounds quickly

Super Suit Features

* Integrated communications (helmet)
* Mini chemical lab (purse)
* Delivery system called chem-balls, which contain chemical concoctions that create things like:
    * hardening foam to halt movement
    * cushioning foam to break falls
    * blinding light and smokescreens to camouflage
    * acid to melt metal
    * ice to freeze or engulf enemies

	AVERAGE		SUPER		EXCEPTIONAL
Intelligence					
Strength					
Durability					
Speed					
Energy					CHEMICAL
Fighting					
Utility					

WASABI

The Power

Abilities

* Precision laser handling
* Professional-level athleticism

ワサビ

Super Suit Features

* Integrated communications (helmet)
* Plasma blades (gauntlets)

	AVERAGE		SUPER	EXCEPTIONAL
Intelligence				
Strength				
Durability				
Speed				
Energy				PLASMA
Fighting				
Utility				

ビッグ・ヒーロー6

フレッド

Abilities

* Encyclopedic comic-book knowledge
* Keen understanding of super villains
* Unbridled enthusiasm

Super Suit Features

* Integrated communications (Kaiju head)
* Endo- and exoskeletons enable super-jumping
* Flamethrower (installed behind mouth of suit)
* Claws
* Flame-resistant

	AVERAGE	SUPER	EXCEPTIONAL
Intelligence	■		
Strength	■	■	
Durability	■	■	■
Speed	■	■	JUMPING
Energy	■	■	FIRE
Fighting	■	■	
Utility	■		

YOKAI

The Villain

Who Is Yokai?

* Mysterious bad guy
* Commands huge swarm of microbots
* Attacks Big Hero 6 team (motive unknown)
* Threatens safety and security of San Fransokyo
* Yokai means "bad guy" or "ghost"

近未来アクション

ロボット工学の天才少年ヒロが繰り広げるアクション・アドベンチャーです。めまぐるしく変わるハイテク都市、サンフランソーキョーを破壊しようとする謎の計画に、ヒロは巻き込まれていきます。ヒロは看護ロボット、ベイマックスの助けのもと、これまで闘った経験もない仲間たちと協力しながら、世界を守ることを決意します。

ビッグ・ヒーロー6

microbot was leading. He headed out the door and down the street. The vibration grew stronger. He smiled. Maybe they weren't too late after all!

He stared down at the petri dish, following the movements of the microbot as if it were a compass. The vibrations were getting stronger with every step he took. Now he knew they were going in the right direction. He was ready to start running when he was yanked from behind by his hoodie. He fell backward and turned to see Baymax.

"Always wait one hour after eating before swimming," Baymax cautioned.

"What?" Hiro said, then looked down and saw that his next step was going to be right into the San Fransokyo Bay! He hadn't realized he'd been walking on a pier for the last few minutes.

Hiro stared out at the cold, dark water. A layer of fog was floating above the bay. He looked at the petri dish again. The microbot was still tapping in the direction of the water, but Hiro didn't see anything out there.

Suddenly, the microbot tapped so hard, the top of the petri dish flew off. Hiro watched the bot disappear into the fog. Then he heard an ominous buzz, soft at first, but gradually getting louder. Slowly a shape emerged. It was the man in the white-and-red Kabuki mask!

Hiro quickly grabbed Baymax and they hid behind a shipping container. He peeked out to see the masked man being transported across the water on a platform—made of a million microbots!

They also seemed to be carrying a strange metal piece. Hiro narrowed his eyes, making out a faint image etched on its side. It looked like an imprint of a bird.

"Your heart rate has increased dramatically," said Baymax.

"Shhh. Okay, Baymax?" Hiro whispered, wanting to stay hidden. "Time to use those upgrades."

Just then, a car came screeching down the street. It drove straight at them! Pressed flat against the container, Hiro and Baymax froze. But they were caught in the headlights.

ビッグ・ヒーロー・6

Chapter 16

The car skidded to a stop. When Hiro saw who was driving, he blinked a couple of times and smacked himself in the head. Wasabi was the driver! The rest of the group was jammed in to the car with him.

"Hiro?" Wasabi said.

"No, no, no! Get out of here! Go!" Hiro yelled, knowing they had no idea what danger they were walking into. He couldn't figure out why they were there in the first place. Then he looked at Baymax and remembered. The big robot had contacted his friends to improve his health.

Wasabi climbed out of the car. "Dude, what are you doing here?" He looked around at the grimy docks.

"Nothing. I'm fine," Hiro whispered as they all climbed out of the car.

But Wasabi was staring at the robot. "Is that Baymax?"

Hiro moved quickly to his friend and tried to push him back toward the vehicle. "Yeah, but you really—"

Go Go asked, "Uh, why is Baymax wearing carbon-fiber underpants?"

"I also know karate," Baymax said.

Hiro took a deep breath. "You guys need to go, okay?"

"No," Honey said. "Don't . . . don't push us away. We're here for you."

Baymax nodded. "Those who suffer a loss require support from friends and loved ones. Who would like to share their feelings first?"

Hiro cringed as Fred said, "I'll go. Okay, my name is Fred, and it has been thirty days since my last—" He stopped, staring up at something above their heads. "Holy mother of Megazon!" he said as the shipping container behind them began to rise.

It was being lifted by microbots!

Then the masked man from the warehouse appeared directly behind the container.

"Am I the only one seeing this?" Fred shouted.

Honey raised her phone and quickly took a photo. The flash blinded the villain for a second.

Then, furious, he hurled the shipping container at them.

The friends scrambled out of the way as Baymax jumped up and caught the falling container.

"Go! Baymax, get him!" Hiro cheered. Go Go grabbed Hiro's arm and pulled him into Wasabi's car.

"No! What are you doing?" Hiro yelled as they all piled in behind him. "Baymax can handle that guy!"

THUMP! Something had hit the car roof. It was Baymax.

"Oh, no," Baymax said.

Baymax's rear end was wedged in the sunroof when Wasabi floored it. The car zoomed away from the pier with the masked man and the microbots right behind it.

Go Go narrowed her eyes. "Hiro. Explanation. Now."

"He stole my microbots! He started the fire! I don't know who he is!" Hiro said as a swarm of microbots streamed toward the car.

"Baymax! Palm-heel strike!" Hiro said. Baymax leaned his armored hand out, and when the microbots hit it, they scattered in every direction.

The car swerved off course.

"Hard left!" Go Go shouted, and they turned a corner with tires squealing.

Fred suddenly brightened like a bulb. "The mask . . . the black suit . . . we are under attack from a super villain, people! A real bad guy— a Yokai! I mean, how cool is that?" he said as the car whipped around a corner and jolted to a stop.

"Why are we stopped?" Go Go asked.

"The light's red!" Wasabi exclaimed.

Everyone groaned.

"There are no red lights in a car chase!" Go Go screamed.

Wasabi nodded and gunned it. Then he leaned out the window, looked toward Yokai, and yelled, "Why are you trying to kill us?"

Yokai hurled a car at them in response. Terrified, Wasabi clicked on his turn signal and screeched around a corner.

Go Go was furious. "Did you just put your blinker on?"

Wasabi cringed. "You have to indicate your turn! It's the law!"

Go Go couldn't take another second. She took out her gum, stuck it on the dashboard, pushed back Wasabi's seat, and slid onto his lap. She grabbed the wheel and slammed on the gas pedal with her foot. The car hurtled forward.

Hiro moved to take Go Go's spot in the front seat, yelling, "Stop! Baymax can take this guy!" But the passenger door suddenly swung open, and out tumbled Hiro.

Baymax grabbed Hiro's hoodie seconds before he hit the pavement. "Seat belts save lives," Baymax said. "Buckle up every time!"

Go Go looked into the rearview mirror. There was nothing behind them. For a moment, it seemed Yokai and the microbots had given up. Go Go smiled—then saw that she was driving on a ramp formed by millions of microbots!

Before she knew it, the ramp turned into a tunnel that was closing around them. Up ahead, the tunnel's exit was closing fast!

Wasabi threw his hands over his eyes as Go Go zoomed toward the tunnel's exit. Hiro braced himself and yelled, "Baymax, hold on!"

"We're not going to make it!" Wasabi howled. But Go Go steered the car onto the wall of the tunnel, lifted into a one-sided wheelie, and squeezed the car through the tunnel's narrowing exit.

"Aaaah!" everyone yelled as the car went sailing.

"We made it!" Wasabi cheered. But his relief

turned to horror when he saw that the tunnel's exit was right over the bay. Everyone screamed as the car splashed nose first into the water and started sinking.

Filling with water, the car began to sink. Yokai watched and waited until it disappeared. Then he and the microbots retreated into the darkness.

Chapter 17

Inside the car, the friends struggled to escape. They were losing air quickly. But just when things were looking hopeless, a big hand pulled them from their seats. Baymax had removed his body armor and inflated to a larger size than he had ever been before. Wrapping his arms around them, he floated everyone to the surface.

Baymax bobbed onto his back and placed the friends, gasping for air, on his stomach.

"I told you we'd make it!" Honey exclaimed.

"Your injuries require my attention," Baymax told them. "And your body temperatures are low."

Hiro agreed. "We should get out of here."

"I know a place," Fred said.

They settled themselves on Baymax for the ride to the dock. Go Go saw her gum float to the surface and happily popped it back into her mouth.

Within an hour, Hiro and his friends were standing in front of a large mansion in San Fransokyo's most exclusive suburb. They looked around, confused. What was Fred up to?

"Where are we?" Honey asked, pushing her wet hair out of her face.

"And where are you going?" Hiro asked with a shiver as Fred went up the front steps.

"Welcome to *mi casa*," Fred said finally. "That's French for 'front door.'" He pressed the doorbell.

"Listen, nitwit, a lunatic in a mask just tried to kill us. So I'm not in the mood for any—" Go Go said, stopping midsentence as the door was pulled open by a butler!

"Welcome home, Master Frederick," he said in a British accent.

"Heathcliff, my man!" Fred greeted the butler with a fist bump before turning and addressing everyone else. "Come on in, guys! We'll be safe here."

Baymax noticed Fred's greeting and fist-bumped the butler, too. "Bata-lata-la."

The friends walked into the vast entryway, stunned. "Freddie," Honey said, "this is your house?"

"I thought you lived under a bridge," Go Go said.

Fred shrugged. "Well, technically, it belongs to my parents. They're on vacay on the family island."

He led them into his enormous bedroom. It was

a virtual museum of rare comic books, Japanese monsters called Kaiju, and sci-fi action figures. A huge painting of Fred dressed like a barbarian riding a white tiger hung on the wall.

Wasabi stared up at the painting wide-eyed. "If I hadn't just been attacked by a guy in a Kabuki mask, I think this would be the weirdest thing I've seen today."

The friends settled into comfortable chairs while Baymax tended to their cuts and bruises. Hiro grabbed a notepad and started to sketch. "Your body temperature is still low," Baymax told him.

Baymax leaned against Hiro's back and began to glow red. Heat emanated from his body. One by one, the friends were drawn to his warmth. Fred wrapped his arms around Baymax and laid his head on Baymax's back.

"Ahh. It's like spooning a warm marshmallow."

"So nice," Honey said with a smile.

Hiro's sketch turned into a picture of a bird, the image he had seen on the metal structure the microbots had been carrying. "Does this symbol mean anything to you guys?" he asked.

"Yes!" Fred said. "It's a bird!"

Hiro looked at Fred and sighed. "Yokai was carrying something with my microbots. This symbol was on it," he explained, hoping it was a clue to who might be behind the Kabuki mask. But for now it seemed like a dead end.

"Apprehending the man in the Kabuki mask will improve Hiro's emotional state," Baymax said.

"Apprehend him?" Go Go asked. "We don't even know who he is."

"I have a theory!" Fred said, and ran to his carefully archived comics collection. He held up a comic book and showed them a masked super villain. "Dr. Sinister?" he asked the group. Fred frowned and turned the page. "Actually, millionaire weapons designer Malcolm Chazzeltick!" Then he held up another comic. "The Annihilator?" Fred asked, and shook his head. He showed one last picture. "Behind the mask, wealthy industrialist Reid Axworthy!"

Fred ran to his computer and pressed a key. "Don't you guys get it? The man in the mask, our Yokai, is none other than"—the group gathered around as Fred hit another key—"high-tech tycoon Alistair Krei!"

"What?" Hiro said.

Fred nodded. "Think about it. Krei wanted your microbots, and you said no. Rules don't apply to a man like Krei!"

Hiro sighed. He was going to need more evidence than a guess from Fred in order to believe that the richest man in the world was also a crazed criminal. "There's no way. The guy's kind of high-profile."

"Then who was the guy in the mask?" Honey asked.

Hiro didn't have an answer. "I don't know," he said. "I don't know anything about him." He looked over to Baymax, who suddenly displayed Yokai's vital signs on his chest screen.

"His blood type is AB negative. Cholesterol levels elevated. Blood pressure one thirty—" Baymax said.

"Baymax, you scanned him?" Hiro asked, unable to contain his excitement.

The robot nodded. "I am programmed to assess everyone's health-care needs."

Hiro jumped up. "I can use the data from your scan to find him!"

Go Go was skeptical. She snapped her gum. "You'd have to scan everyone in San Fransokyo— that might take . . . forever. "

Hiro sighed. He knew she was right. He began to pace. "No, no, no, no. There's always a work-around." With his fingers, he tapped his head, trying to force an idea to come. And then he saw one of Fred's toys.

"I'll scan the whole city at the same time. I just have to upgrade Baymax's sensor."

He looked from Baymax to his friends. "Actually, I need to upgrade all of you if we're gonna catch this guy," Hiro said, ready to head back to his garage.

Wasabi said, "Upgrade *us*? What are you talking about? We can't go against that guy. We're nerds!"

Honey approached the subject more calmly. "Hiro, of course we want to help, but he has all those microbots, and we're just . . . we're just us."

"No," he said, "you can be way more." Hiro looked up at the superhero art in Fred's room, and his mind swam with ideas. *Yeah*, Hiro thought, *way better upgrades!*

Fred said, "Can you feel it? Our origin story begins!" He was giddy with delight. "We're gonna be *superheroes*!"

ビッグ・ヒーロー6

Chapter 18

Hiro and the group gathered up the projects they had made at SFIT and brought them to Hiro's garage.

"We're never going to catch this guy unless we can take out the microbots. So we need to level the playing field," Hiro said.

He looked at Go Go's bike, Wasabi's laser, Honey's chemical concoctions, and Fred's Kaiju costume. "Yep," Hiro said. "We can work with this."

Hiro had them all stand in front of the garage door. "Arms up," he directed before running a scanner over them. "The neural transmitter must be in his mask. We get the mask and he can't control the bots. Game over."

Hiro rolled his chair to his computer workstation. Baymax watched over him as he worked late into the night. Hiro had six screens going in order to modify and design all the new gear. The 3-D printer was working overtime printing out sleek armor for everyone. Each member of the team worked hard, dismantling and redesigning their tech. Hiro worked with everyone on the improvements.

When they were done, Hiro and his friends took their tech out to Fred's estate, where they could refine their new skills. Within the walls of the private garden, Fred set the mood by placing a Kabuki mask on Heathcliff.

Then they all suited up. They looked like they belonged in Fred's collection of superhero action figures.

Honey was thrilled with her new pink body armor. She thought it complemented her blue eyes. Then she looked at her shiny new chem purse. "Oh, I love it! I love it! I love it!" she said. Suddenly, a pink chem-ball popped out and Honey caught it.

"Give it a try," Hiro said, so she tossed it at Heathcliff. The butler was instantly covered in sticky pink goo. Honey clapped her hands.

Go Go was wowed by her new gear, too. Her yellow mag-lev wheels were modified into discs to fit her feet instead of her bike. This gave her the hyperspeed she'd always dreamed of as she skated along. There were also yellow discs on her arms, which were powerful weapons that could be thrown to cut through anything in her path.

"Got to say, I like it!" Go Go said.

"Take it slow," Hiro warned.

Go Go pinwheeled her arms a bit, then found her balance and zoomed around the hedges. She grabbed a garden hose and coiled it around Heathcliff, immobilizing the butler in a flash.

Hiro smiled and put the head of a Kaiju suit on Fred to complete his armor.

"Whoa! This is awesome!" Fred said. He bent his knees and felt himself bounce. Then he took a giant leap, shouting, "Super-jump!"

"And there's one more thing," Hiro said while a flame jetted from Fred's Kaiju jaws.

"I breathe fire!" Fred shouted. He blasted a ring of fire onto the grass around Heathcliff, who seemed to barely notice. Fred was so happy, he nearly cried. "This is the best day of my life," he told Hiro.

In another part of the garden, wearing his green armor, Wasabi was trying to get comfortable with his new gloves. They were equipped with high-powered retractable lasers that could slice through anything.

Wasabi was terrified of them.

He held them away from his body as he approached a decorative marble pillar. He closed his eyes, and with a single swipe, sliced the pillar in two. He opened his eyes and smiled. "Whoa! Laser hands!"

Hiro smiled. "Guys, I'd like to introduce . . . Baymax: Mark 2."

The friends stared up at the huge robot in awe.

Hiro had designed Baymax's bright red body armor in a way that amplified his stature and strength. With a purple ribbed midsection that allowed him to bend, he made a powerful impression.

"Ah. He's glorious!" Fred exclaimed.

Then Honey gathered everyone around Baymax for a quick selfie.

Hiro smiled. "Show 'em what you got, buddy."

They stared at Baymax, but the big robot didn't seem to understand.

"The fist!" Hiro said to him. "Show them the fist."

Baymax reached out for a fist bump. "Bata-lata . . ."

"No, not that," Hiro said. "You know? The thing . . . the other thing."

Baymax held out his arm and his giant red

fist shot out like a rocket. It destroyed a huge flowerpot, then smashed through the garden wall.

"Whoa!" was all the team could say.

"My hand is gone." Baymax stared at the wisps of smoke where his hand used to be. Just then, the fist returned to Baymax's arm. "It is back," he said.

"Rocket fist make Freddie so happy!" Fred squealed.

Hiro nodded. "That's only one of his new upgrades. Baymax, wings!" Baymax's fixed carbon-fiber wings deployed.

"No way," Fred said, dropping his jaw.

"Thrusters," Hiro directed.

"I fail to see how flying makes me a better health-care companion," Baymax said.

"I fail to see how you fail to see that it's awesome." Hiro climbed on Baymax's back. He locked on to Baymax with magnetic knee pads and gloves that were part of his own black-and-purple armor. And his helmet allowed him to communicate with all the members of the team. "Full thrust!"

Baymax and Hiro took off, but Baymax seemed to have trouble rising into the air. They hit the ground, nearly clobbering the team.

As Baymax and Hiro took off again, the group held its breath. This time Baymax was a little steadier.

Hiro realized they all needed time to sharpen their new skills. And he was right. With some practice, Fred was jumping and shooting flames at targets with absolute precision. Out on Fred's tennis court, Wasabi began knocking tennis balls out of the air with ease—and they were perfectly sliced in two. Go Go was throwing her discs with lightning speed and control. Honey had mastered the art of launching the chem-balls so that they always hit their mark.

And eventually, Baymax flew through the air like a pro with Hiro on his back. So Hiro decided it was time to really crank it up. He rocketed Baymax over the city, barrel-rolled and banked sharply left, then right, weaving through a tunnel, over and under neon signs. They flew past a high-rise that reflected their own image back at them. It was incredible. Hiro couldn't help yelling, "Yeah!"

Baymax told him, "Your neurotransmitter levels are rising steadily."

"Which means what?" Hiro asked.

"The treatment is working," Baymax explained. Hiro could feel it, too. For the first time since Tadashi's death, he was happy.

Chapter 19

In order to optimize Baymax's scan range, he and Hiro flew up to the top of a tall wind turbine that overlooked the city.

Hiro couldn't stop thinking of their amazing flight. "Wow. That was . . . that was . . ."

"Sick," Baymax finished his sentence.

Hiro looked at him in surprise. "It is just an expression," Baymax said.

The boy couldn't help but laugh. "Yeah, that's right, buddy."

The view from the top of the wind turbine was stunning. They could see the whole city and even parts beyond the bay that surrounded it. Hiro sighed at the beauty. "I am never taking a bus again."

Baymax turned to Hiro and blinked. "Your emotional state has improved."

Hiro frowned, surprised by the comment.

"I can deactivate if you say you are satisfied with your care."

"What? No, I don't want you to deactivate!" Hiro exclaimed. "We still have to find that guy. So fire up that super sensor."

New lenses dropped over Baymax's eyes. He scanned the entire city, gathering readings on hundreds of thousands of people and eliminating those that didn't match Yokai's profile. "Functionality improved. One thousand percent increase in range," Baymax said. "But there is no match in San Fransokyo."

Hiro was disappointed for a moment, then—

"I *have* found a match on that island." Baymax pointed to the bay. Hiro looked up at Baymax's digital medical readout. It was blinking MATCH.

"Akuma Island!" Hiro exclaimed.

That night, they all jumped on Baymax's back. He deployed his red carbon-fiber wings. He wasn't used to the weight of the whole team on his back and wobbled a bit as he took off.

"Killer view," Go Go commented, as if she spent every day skimming the water of the bay on the back of a robot.

"Yeah," Wasabi agreed, his voice wavering slightly. "If I wasn't terrified of heights, I'd probably love this. But I'm terrified of heights, so I don't love it."

Fred was his usual overeager self. "I can't believe this. We're going to bring an evildoer to justice! In cool outfits! I mean, we're superheroes!"

His statement made Wasabi frown. "We're not superheroes," he corrected Fred. "We're nerds."

Flying only inches above the water, they got closer to Akuma Island. Hiro found an empty stretch of land. "There, Baymax. Take us in."

The robot turned and landed near a group of military-type buildings.

"Awesome!" Fred said. "Our first landing as a team!"

Everyone scrambled to their feet. "Guys, come on," Hiro called, leading them toward a concrete bunker.

But Wasabi was staring at a sign on a nearby fence. "Quarantine? Do you know what 'quarantine' means?" he asked in a trembling voice.

Baymax turned and said, "Quarantine: enforced isolation to prevent the spread of contamination."

Wasabi rolled his eyes and threw his hands up. "I know what it means!" he shouted. "Tell *them*!"

They ignored Wasabi and approached a large steel door. "Be ready," Hiro whispered. "He could be anywhere."

Just then, a twig snapped behind them!

Instantly, they spun around and unleashed their weapons. Honey threw a dozen chem-balls, while Fred shot a huge breath of fire. Go Go threw one of her discs, and Hiro ducked out of the way. Wasabi windmilled his laser blades, and Baymax struck a karate pose.

"Did I get it?" Wasabi cried.

As the smoke cleared, the team looked into the haze and saw a seagull staring back at them. It shook its head and flew off into the night.

"Well, there goes the element of surprise," Go Go said, picking up the discs she'd thrown.

"Well, at least we know our gear works," Honey declared as Baymax reached over to extinguish a fire on Hiro's helmet with his fingers.

Wasabi stepped up and cut through the door with his laser blades. The team hesitated for a moment. They knew once they stepped inside, the game was on. They peeked in and saw a stairwell that led down into blackness.

Chapter 20

Sticking close together, the team crept down the stairwell.

Fred chose that time to begin singing. "Six intrepid friends led by Fred, their leader. Fred. Fred's Angels. Uh-uh-uh. Fred's Angels. Uh-uh-uh. Harnessing the power of the sun with the ancient amulet they found in the attic. Uh-uh-uh. The amulet is green. Uh-uh-uh. It's probably an emerald. Uh-uh-uh—"

Wasabi silenced him with a look. "Fred, I will laser-hand you in the face!"

Fred shrank back.

"Shhh," Hiro said as they entered a huge concrete testing lab. "Any sign of him, Baymax?" He looked at Baymax's scanner. The signal had disappeared.

"This structure is interfering with my sensor,"

Baymax said, still trying to get a reading.

"Oh, great," Wasabi said anxiously. "The robot's broken."

"Guys, you might want to see this . . . ," Honey said.

Everyone was on high alert as they scanned the lab. The place appeared to have been badly damaged. The ceiling had caved in, leaving a gaping hole. The walls were cracked, and chunks of concrete were scattered everywhere.

Two large circular structures that vaguely resembled portals of some sort dominated the room. One was intact but half dismantled. The other seemed to have been completely blown up.

"What do you think they are, genius?" Go Go asked Hiro.

"I'm not sure. But look," Hiro replied, pointing to a bird symbol on one of them. It was the same one Hiro had seen on the metal piece Yokai was transporting across the bay.

Then Honey said, "Hiro." She was pointing to a flickering light. It was coming from a control room in a tower overlooking the lab floor.

Yokai must be up there, Hiro thought.

The team climbed a decrepit metal stairway, ready for battle. But when they burst into the control room, they found it abandoned.

The flickering light was coming from a bank

of video screens. The biggest screen showed the graphic image of a bird. SILENT SPARROW was printed underneath it.

Hiro walked over to the computer and hit a key. An image of Alistair Krei appeared.

"Krei . . . ," Hiro said, a little shocked.

The paused video began to play. It showed Alistair Krei standing in the lab when it was sleek and new. A small audience that included military officials was listening as Krei said, "We were asked to do the impossible. And that's what we did. We've reinvented the very concept of transportation."

Krei gave his audience a broad smile and pointed to two large circular structures—the same ones the team had found in the lab. "Friends, I present Project Silent Sparrow." He nodded to the control booth, and the two structures powered up with a hum.

Krei took the hat of one of the generals. "May I?" he asked. But before the general could answer, Krei tossed the hat into the closest circular portal. In less than a second, it flew out of the other portal.

"Whoa! A magic hat!" Fred said.

"No," Hiro said, impressed with what Krei had done. "Teleportation. Those circles are portals."

On the video, Krei handed the general his hat. "Teleportation: the transport of matter instantaneously through space. Not science fiction anymore," Krei said. The guests burst into applause.

Next, Krei led his audience up to the control room. "Now, we didn't spend billions of dollars to teleport hats." His guests nodded and laughed nervously as Krei motioned to a video monitor. "Ladies and gentlemen, you're here to witness history."

Krei spoke into a microphone. The image of a young woman flashed onto the screen. "Ready to go for a ride, Abigail?" he asked.

The pilot gave a thumbs-up. "We've invited all these people; might as well give them a show," she said as she climbed into a flight pod set up to enter one of the portals.

Krei turned to his guests. "The first human teleportation in history, courtesy of Krei Tech Industries," he said with a flourish, and the countdown began.

Chapter 21

Hiro and the team watched the video as the flight pod's engines fired up. The portal was humming. A computer-generated voice echoed through the lab: "T-minus thirty seconds to launch."

"All systems go for pod launch," Krei said.

A technician suddenly said, "Sir, we've picked up a slight irregularity in the field harmonics."

"Huh," Krei said, looking at the readout on the screen.

One of the generals stepped forward. "Mr. Krei, is there a problem?"

"No, no, problem," Krei said with a wave of his hand. "It's well within the parameters. Let's move forward," he said to the technician.

"Five, four, three, two ... one," the voice said. "Pod engaged." And the pod shot into the first portal, but the moment it entered, alarms screamed.

"We've lost all contact with the pilot!" a technician yelled. When the second portal exploded, Krei's audience scrambled out of the way.

"Oh, no," Honey said as they all watched the technicians panic. They understood that the pilot now had no way of exiting the portal.

The video was becoming shaky. A spinning vortex was forming at the center of the first portal. It was growing stronger and stronger. Items in the lab began flying into it. Suddenly, the vortex became strong enough to pull the concrete from the walls. The place was going to implode!

"The pilot is gone!" a technician yelled.

"Krei, shut it down! Now!" the general shouted just as Krei hit a kill switch.

The video screen in front of the friends went black.

Hiro stared numbly at the screen. Now he understood why the lab was destroyed. He figured the government must have taken over Krei's equipment after the disaster.

"Krei's using my microbots to steal his machine back. But why?" Hiro asked.

Suddenly, a familiar sound drew everyone's attention to the lab. It was the sound of buzzing microbots—millions of them! Hiro looked out the control room window. The white-and-red face of Yokai came into view. He was standing on a platform of microbots.

They watched the black-cloaked figure raise his arm and the microbots hurled a chunk of debris at the control tower.

The debris smashed into the tower's base. Hiro and his team held on as the tower buckled and swayed. A final wave of microbots leveled the entire structure.

Yokai smiled as he watched tons of rubble thunder to the floor. There was no way anyone could have survived.

ビッグ・ヒーロー6

◄ Chapter 22 ►

Yokai turned his attention back to the business at hand—moving the precious portal. He used the microbots to dismantle the last portions of it.

Meanwhile, under the control tower wreckage, Hiro and his buddies huddled beneath Baymax. His huge carbon-fiber-covered body had protected them from the falling debris. Hiro gave Baymax a nudge. "Get us out of here!"

Yokai was ready to command the bots to raise the portal up through the hole in the lab's ceiling. Then—*smash!* Baymax's armored fist came crashing through the control room wreckage. Yokai spun around and saw Baymax throwing off steel beams and chunks of cement. He was stunned to see Hiro and the team come out from the wreckage.

Yokai suddenly realized he had to deal with this

annoying team of misfits before he could get the portal to safety.

Hiro and the others came at Yokai with everything they had. "Go for the transmitter behind the mask!" Hiro yelled.

But before Baymax could make a move, a wave of microbots knocked him back. Hiro ran to help him, leaving the remaining team face to face with Yokai.

"All right, what's the plan?" Wasabi asked.

Fred leaped over Yokai. "Super-jump!" he yelled. "Gravity crush! Falling hard!" he narrated as Yokai swatted him away with a wave of microbots.

"Seriously, what's the plan?" Wasabi called.

"Go for the mask," Go Go instructed.

"Right behind you!" Honey replied. The two of them took off together.

Go Go rode up a wall and flung her discs at Yokai. But Yokai dodged one while he deflected another. The discs flew past Yokai, just missing Honey as she lobbed a chem-ball. The chem-ball created an ice patch that caused Go Go to slip. She skidded on the ice and slammed into Honey, knocking them both down.

Yokai turned to Wasabi. Wasabi did his best to sound brave. "You want to dance, masked man? 'Cause you'll be dancing with these!" He waved his laser hands. "Hand over the mask, or you'll get a taste of THIS! And a little bit of THAT! Ha-ha!"

Yokai threw a cloud of microbots at Wasabi. When Wasabi slashed at them wildly, the microbots seemed to scatter. Wasabi was thrilled. Then he looked down and saw that the swarm was covering his feet and climbing his legs. They lifted him off the ground and threw him into Fred. Fred unleashed a stream of fire that sprayed like an out-of-control garden hose as Wasabi knocked him to the floor.

Yokai was pleased. Most of the team was now out of commission. He turned his attention back to re-forming the microbot platform and raising the portal out of the roof. The job was almost done when Hiro, riding on Baymax, flew at him full force. Hiro was dismayed to see his friends all knocked out of the fight. They were a team, but they weren't fighting like one.

Yokai angrily sent a stream of microbots at Baymax and knocked him back. The jolt sent Hiro flying forward, slamming him into Yokai. As Hiro and Yokai tumbled down, Yokai's Kabuki mask flew off. All the microbots instantly fell to the ground.

"It's over, Krei!" Hiro said.

Yokai had his back to Hiro. But when he turned, Hiro's eyes grew wide in disbelief.

Chapter 23

"Professor Callaghan!" Hiro said, confused. The team was starting to recover and was now standing next to Hiro. "But . . . the explosion. You died," Hiro said.

"No, your microbots kept me safe," Callaghan replied.

Hiro's mind was racing. "But Tadashi . . . you just let him die?"

"Give me the mask, Hiro," the professor said.

"He went in there to save you!" Hiro said.

"That was his mistake!" Callaghan replied.

Wrong answer! Hiro thought, and something in him snapped. "Baymax!" he said, gritting his teeth. "Destroy!"

"My programming prevents me from injuring a human being," Baymax said.

"Not anymore," Hiro replied as he touched

Baymax's chest and opened his access panel.

Baymax tried to reason with him. "Hiro, this is not what—"

But Hiro wouldn't listen. He pulled out Tadashi's nurse chip. "Do it, Baymax. Destroy him!"

"No!" Go Go shouted. "Stop!"

Baymax raised his rocket fist, and Callaghan backed away.

But just as Baymax was about to launch, Go Go plowed into him. The blow redirected the fist, which hit a cement wall. It missed Callaghan by only a few feet.

Baymax then raised his fist and pointed it at Go Go. "Get the nurse chip back into Baymax!" she yelled.

Honey grabbed the chip off the ground and tossed it to Go Go, who zoomed over to Baymax and jammed the chip into his access panel. Baymax's rocket fist powered down.

"What are you doing?" Hiro called. "He's getting away!"

Callaghan had gotten the mask containing the neural transmitter back on. He directed the microbots to grab the last pieces of the portal. Moments later, he had gone through the hole in the ceiling.

Baymax blinked at the destruction around

him. "My health-care protocol has been violated," he said. "I regret any distress I may have caused."

Hiro, angry and frustrated, looked at his team. "How could you do that? I had him!" he shouted.

"What you just tried to do, we never signed up for," Wasabi said.

Go Go nodded. "We said we'd catch the guy. That's it."

"I never should have let you help me," Hiro said as he climbed on Baymax's back. "Baymax, find Callaghan."

"My enhanced scanner has been damaged," Baymax replied.

Hiro groaned in frustration. "Wings," he commanded.

As Baymax's wings deployed, Fred said, "Hiro, this isn't part of the plan."

But Hiro ignored him. "Fly!" he said to Baymax, and the team watched as they flew out of the building and streaked across the sky toward San Fransokyo.

ビッグ・ヒーロー6

Back at his garage, Hiro burst in with Baymax behind him. He sat down at his computer and accessed Baymax's super sensor. This enabled him to make code changes directly into Baymax.

Baymax stared at Hiro. Hiro's eyebrows were furrowed as he concentrated on the programming. "Your blood pressure is elevated. You appear to be distressed," Baymax said.

"I'm fine," Hiro snapped, typing faster. "There." He turned to Baymax. "Is it working?"

"My sensor is now operational," Baymax replied.

"Good," Hiro said, and tapped the access port on Baymax's chest. But the port didn't open. Hiro tapped it again. "What?"

"Are you going to remove my health-care chip?" asked Baymax.

"Yes. Open," Hiro said, tapping the port again.

"But my purpose is to heal the sick and injured."

"Baymax, open your access port," Hiro ordered.

"Will terminating Callaghan improve your emotional state?" Baymax asked.

"Yes! No. . . . I don't know!" Hiro said. He removed Baymax's chest armor to get to the port, but it still wouldn't open.

Hiro tapped it harder.

"Is this what Tadashi would have wanted?" Baymax asked, and Hiro felt a bit of a sting.

"It doesn't matter," Hiro said angrily, although he suddenly began to feel conflicted.

"Tadashi programmed me to aid—"

But before Baymax could finish, Hiro said, "Tadashi is gone." Then he dropped his head against Baymax's chest. "Tadashi is gone."

"Tadashi is here," Baymax said.

Suddenly, Hiro heard the muffled sound of Tadashi's voice. He looked up at Baymax in disbelief. Baymax was running the data from the first day he was activated.

"This is Tadashi Hamada," the muffled voice said, "and this is the first test of my robotics project."

Hiro could see his brother on Baymax's display screen. He watched as Tadashi ran test after test, trying to create Baymax. Finally, on his eighty-fourth try, the big white robot next to Tadashi said, "Hello. I am Baymax, your personal health-care companion."

Hiro watched Tadashi pump his fist and spin around in his chair. "It works! He works! Ah! Yes! This is amazing! You work!" Tadashi cheered. "I can't believe it! Ha-ha!"

A bittersweet smile came over Hiro's face as he watched his brother. Then Tadashi said, "Okay. All right. Big moment here." He turned toward Baymax, fingers crossed. "Okay. Scan me."

On the screen, Baymax stared at Tadashi. "Your neurotransmitter levels are elevated. This indicates you are very happy."

Tadashi said, "I am. I really am! Wait till my brother sees you!"

A tear ran down Hiro's cheek.

"You're going to help so many people, buddy. So many," Tadashi said. "That's all for now. I am satisfied with my care."

And with that, Baymax's display screen froze on the image of Tadashi. Hiro touched the screen.

"Thank you," Hiro said, looking up at Baymax. He didn't need to ask him to open his access port anymore.

Then Hiro heard someone call his name. He turned and saw the whole team standing in the doorway of his garage. By the looks on their faces,

Hiro knew they'd seen Tadashi's video, too. Hiro hung his head. "Guys, I . . . I'm . . . ," he said.

Go Go rushed up to him. "We're going to catch Callaghan. And we're going to make it right," she said as she hugged Hiro. The rest of the team watched, a little stunned. Was Go Go actually hugging someone?

"But maybe don't leave your team stranded on a spooky island next time," Wasabi said.

"Oh, man," Hiro said, realizing that he'd been wrong to abandon them.

"Nah, it's cool," Fred told Hiro. "Heathcliff picked us up in the family chopper."

"Hiro, we found something you should see," Honey said. She was holding a hard drive.

Hiro hooked it to his computer and saw a frozen image of the test pilot, Abigail, on his screen. As the video played, Hiro gasped. Abigail was standing with Alistair Krei and another man. "Is that . . . Callaghan was there?"

"Yeah, but why?" Go Go asked.

"And they look like they're good friends," Fred added.

Hiro was confused. "But Callaghan hates Krei." He thought back to the time at the Tech Showcase when Callaghan warned him not to take Krei's offer. "I wouldn't trust him with your microbots, or anything else," he had said.

Hiro fast-forwarded to a close-up image of the pilot. He zoomed in. He could clearly see the name on her flight suit. It read CALLAGHAN. "The pilot was Callaghan's daughter. Callaghan blames Krei."

Fred nodded knowingly. "This is a revenge story."

Hiro nodded, too, realizing that Professor Callaghan was after Krei all along. He needed Hiro's microbots to carry out his revenge. Hiro thought about the awful destruction the portal could cause. "So what are we waiting for?" he said to his friends.

The team prepared to head to Krei Tech's new campus, knowing it had to be Professor Callaghan's real target.

Chapter 25

When they arrived, Alistair Krei was addressing his employees at a company-wide meeting outdoors. "This beautiful new campus is the culmination of a lifelong dream," he told them. "But none of this would have been possible without a few bumps in the road. Those setbacks made us stronger and set us on the path to a bright future."

Krei was smiling when a voice boomed, *"Setbacks?"*

It was Yokai. A wave of microbots carried him down the side of a building behind Krei. The crowd panicked and began to run. Krei ran, too, but Yokai swooped him up in a fist of microbots. "Was my daughter just a setback?" he yelled, pushing up the mask for a moment.

"Callaghan!" Krei shouted. "Your daughter . . .

that was an accident!"

"No!" Callaghan yelled as the microbots tightened around Krei. "You knew it was unsafe! My daughter is gone because of your arrogance!"

He raised his arms and wave upon wave of microbots descended on the Krei Tech campus. They carried in sections of the teleportation portal and quickly assembled it. Columns of microbots held the portal suspended over the campus.

"What are you doing?" Krei asked, terrified, as the portal began to hum.

"You took everything from me when you sent Abigail into that machine," Professor Callaghan said. "Now I'm going to take everything from you."

Krei knew all too well what happened when there was no exit portal. All of Krei Tech would be sucked into oblivion!

Callaghan smiled. "You're going to watch everything you've built disappear. And then it's your turn."

He was about to give the signal to take the portal up to full power when he heard a voice call, "Professor Callaghan!"

The professor froze. Hiro and his friends were standing on the roof of a Krei Tech building. "Let him go!" Hiro yelled. "Is this what Abigail would have wanted?"

"Abigail is gone!" Callaghan shouted, his voice full of anguish.

"This won't change anything," Hiro said. "Trust me, I know."

For a brief moment, Callaghan stopped.

"Listen to the kid, Callaghan!" Krei begged. "Let me go and I'll give you anything you want!"

Callaghan looked at Krei and became furious again. "I want my daughter back!" he yelled, lowering his mask, and the microbot fist around Krei squeezed even tighter.

"No!" Hiro shouted, watching Krei's face turn redder and redder.

But Callaghan had heard enough. He activated the portal and sent a wave of microbots to destroy Hiro and the team.

The microbots slammed into them, knocking them off the building's ledge. Fred bounced onto a nearby roof, while Honey deployed a chem-ball net to catch herself, Go Go, and Wasabi. Baymax immediately swooped in to scoop up Hiro.

Hiro climbed onto Baymax's back and flew toward Callaghan. "Go for the mask!" he yelled to Baymax, hoping to get control of the neural transmitter.

But before Baymax and Hiro could reach him, Callaghan used the microbots to grab and throw them. Baymax crashed through the wall of a building, while Hiro broke through a window.

Suddenly, the pull of the portal above him ripped off the ceiling, pulling the debris . . . and Hiro . . . toward it.

Chapter 26

Hiro flailed his arms and grabbed on to the end of a metal pipe. Holding the pipe, Hiro fought against being pulled into the vortex of the portal. He watched his team below, and saw they were being beaten badly.

Yokai laughed as the microbots grabbed Fred's arms and pulled.

"They're tearing me apart!" Fred howled.

Then Yokai turned to Wasabi. He had him pinned between two walls of microbots. "Getting a little tight!" Wasabi said as the walls closed in.

Go Go was immobilized in a ball of microbots. "I could use a little help!" she called.

Everyone seemed to be in a jam, even Honey. She had covered herself in a chemical dome, but the microbots were hammering on it.

Hiro was suddenly frightened. He could see

them losing the battle. They could all be sucked into the portal. As he hung upside down, he watched pieces of debris and loose microbots fall into the gaping maw. "That's it! I know how to beat him!"

He yelled into his communicator, "Hey! Listen up! Use those big brains to think your way out! There are no dead ends!"

It was just the jolt of inspiration the team needed.

Fred grabbed a fallen sign. Spinning the sign, he sliced through the microbots that were holding his Kaiju suit. "Oh, it's Fred time!" he howled. "And we don't need a super suit for the super sign-spin!"

At the same time, Go Go revved her wheels until they smoked—and sliced through the sphere of microbots around her.

Held between two walls of bots, Wasabi knew the best way to escape was to go down. Using his laser hands, he dug through the floor and was free. Honey latched on to a string of microbots that had penetrated her dome. They pulled her to freedom.

But the robot was still surrounded. "Baymax!" Hiro called. He gasped as a sharp piece of debris flew past and cut him.

Baymax looked up, and the two stared at one another before Baymax was completely covered with microbots. Hiro gasped, and then he felt his hands slip on the pipe.

Suddenly, Baymax's rocket fist shot out of a mound of microbots.

The rest of Baymax caught up to his fist and he grabbed Hiro just as the pipe gave way. Krei and Callaghan could only watch. "I love that robot!" Krei shouted.

With a snarl, Callaghan used the microbots to trap Krei against a billboard. Hiro rode Baymax down to the ground, where the team was ready and waiting for action.

"Here's the plan," Hiro told them as he looked toward Callaghan. "We gotta force him up. Close to the portal. Honey, Fred, can you give us a little cover?"

"Let's do this, Freddie!" Honey shouted.

"Like you have to ask," Fred said as he blew a blast of smoke from his Kaiju nostrils. "Smoke screen!"

"Yes!" Hiro cheered as the two disappeared in the cloud of smoke. "All right, Wasabi, here's what I want you to do—"

"I'm good, man!" Wasabi interrupted. "I don't need a plan. Wasabi is winging it." Wasabi ran in and slashed away at the columns of microbots. Go Go sent discs flying at the columns as well, causing large cracks to appear. Honey threw chem-balls into the cracks. The expanding goo caused the columns to shift.

Hiro smiled. They were finally working together as a team.

Baymax and Hiro flew toward Callaghan, drawing an attack of swirling microbots toward the portal. At the last second, they reversed into a dive, going straight into the microbots, which engulfed them.

Hiro activated Baymax. "Back kick! Knife hand! Roundhouse! Hammer fist!" he called out in quick succession. Baymax went at the microbots with a whirlwind of karate moves.

"This ends now!" Callaghan shouted. With one final push, he threw a swarm of microbots at Hiro and Baymax. But with a mighty blow, Baymax punched thousands of microbots into the portal.

The columns shook and Callaghan staggered. With very few microbots left, he struggled to maintain his balance. "No!"

"It's over, Callaghan!" Hiro shouted. "Hand over the mask."

"Never," Callaghan snarled.

"I thought you'd say that," Hiro said. "Fred?"

Fred leaped at Callaghan. "Fred time!" he called as he grabbed the mask. Instantly, the microbot columns collapsed, sending Krei and Callaghan tumbling toward the ground.

Baymax caught the two men in midair.

Hiro watched the columns of microbots holding the portal come apart. With a great shudder, the whole thing crashed to the ground!

Hiro and his friends cheered. The portal had been destroyed and the microbots were lying in heaps!

But seconds later, it was clear that the broken portal was still active. "It's still on!" Hiro said to Krei. "We have to shut it down!"

The portal was sucking in everything around it. Then, pulsing with light and energy, it began sucking in parts of itself.

"We can't!" Krei cried. "The containment field is failing. The portal's going to tear itself apart."

"We need to get out of here, now!" Hiro shouted. Everyone was turning to run when Hiro looked back and saw Baymax staring at the portal. "Baymax!" he shouted.

"My detector is sensing signs of life," Baymax said.

"What?" Hiro said.

"Coming from there," Baymax replied, pointing

at the portal. "The life signs are female. She appears to be in hypersleep."

Hiro gasped. "Callaghan's daughter!" he said. "She's still alive?"

"Abigail!" Callaghan said. Hiro saw the hope in Callaghan's eyes. Then he looked to his team. He knew if there was a chance she was alive, he had to try to save her. He looked at Baymax. "Let's go get her." He climbed onto the robot's back.

Krei stood next to the team on the ground. He said, "The portal is destabilizing. You don't have much time."

Honey was worried. "Hiro, it's too dangerous."

"She's alive in there," Hiro told his team. "Someone has to help."

The team looked at each other and then back at Hiro and Baymax. They understood that Hiro would always be the person who would offer help. Just as Tadashi had been. "What do you say, buddy?" Hiro asked Baymax with a smile.

"Flying makes me a better health-care companion."

And with that, the team watched Baymax and Hiro rocket into the portal.

Chapter 27

Baymax and Hiro dodged debris as they flew through the swirling portal at high speed. "Look out!" Hiro called when a huge chunk of cement whistled by them.

"I have located the patient." Baymax's sensor was picking up stronger life readings the deeper they traveled into the portal. The pull of the vortex was growing stronger, too. Hiro pointed straight ahead. A shiny object was coming at them fast. It was the pod. Baymax wrapped his arms around it as Hiro climbed on. He wiped off the windshield and saw Abigail's face. Her eyes were closed and her face was pale.

Hiro was relieved to see the faint mist her breathing created on the glass. "C'mon, buddy. Let's get her home."

Using his rocket thrusters, Baymax began to

push the pod out of the portal. Hiro could see the light from the exit up ahead. But a large chunk of debris headed straight for Hiro. Baymax got between Hiro and the flying debris, saving him from the hit, and the debris slammed into Baymax.

"Oh, no," Baymax said as most of the armor broke off his body. He was floating in the whirlwind of the portal, badly damaged.

Hiro reached for him. "Baymax! Grab hold!" he yelled, and they reconnected.

But Baymax had bad news. "My thrusters are inoperable," he said.

Hiro's heart sank. He knew it meant they were stranded.

"There is still a way I can get you both to safety," Baymax said, and he began to fire up his rocket fist. He aimed it toward the exit.

"What about you?" Hiro asked, knowing it was the last bit of power Baymax had left. If he used it, he wouldn't have the power to get himself out. He'd be lost in the vortex forever.

"You are my patient. Your health is my only concern," Baymax said.

"No!" Hiro shouted. "There's got to be another way. I'm not going to leave you here. I'll think of something!"

"Hiro, there is no time," Baymax said.

"Please, no," Hiro begged. "I lost Tadashi. I can't lose you, too."

"Tadashi is not gone," he responded, touching Hiro's chest. "Tadashi is here. I am here."

Tears welled up in Hiro's eyes as the seconds ticked away.

"I cannot deactivate until you say you are satisfied with my care," Baymax said.

Hiro shook his head, and tears fell down his cheeks.

"Hiro, are you satisfied with your care?"

Hiro threw his arms around Baymax and finally said, "I am satisfied with my care."

The two friends hugged for as long as they could. Then Baymax nodded, and Hiro attached his magnets to Abigail's pod. Baymax fully powered-up his rocket fist and, *whoosh*, in an instant, Abigail and Hiro were pushed toward the portal opening.

Hiro looked back. With his rocket fist and the last of his armor gone, Baymax looked just like he did when Hiro first saw him, all soft and marshmallow-white. He watched as his friend faded slowly into the distance. Then he closed his eyes.

ビッグ・ヒーロー6

◄ Chapter 28 ►

The area immediately outside the portal had become completely unstable. The Krei Tech buildings were starting to bend and crack toward it. Krei nervously looked at his watch. Only five seconds until implosion.

There was nothing Hiro's team could do but wait. Then just as the portal began to cave in on itself, the pod came shooting out with Hiro riding on top. He and Abigail safely crashed into a pile of inactive microbots.

"Hiro!" Wasabi cried as the team ran up to him.

"They made it!" Fred cheered. But their faces changed when they saw the rocket fist.

"Baymax?" Wasabi asked. Hiro shook his head.

The lights of police cars and emergency vehicles flashed as they approached the scene. The EMTs removed Abigail from the pod and placed her on a stretcher. "Miss, can you hear me—what is your name?" one of them asked.

"Abigail Callaghan," she responded weakly.

"Okay, Abigail, you are going to be fine. We are taking you to the hospital." The EMTs pushed her stretcher quickly toward the ambulance.

Callaghan, who stood next to a police car, watched his daughter move away. "Abigail . . ."

The following morning, it was all over the news. "A massive clean-up continues today at the headquarters of Krei Tech Industries," one TV anchor reported.

A live video showed several excavators and bulldozers working on the decimated Krei Tech campus. "Reports are still flooding in about a group of unidentified individuals who prevented what could have been a major catastrophe," the anchor said. "The whole city of San Fransokyo is asking: Who are these heroes? And where are they now?"

But Hiro didn't hear the broadcast. He and his friends were heading out of the Lucky Cat Café when they walked by his aunt Cass. "Hey, sweetie!" she called, and they hugged. Then he held his arms out, ready for another. "Last hug," she said, grabbing him close again. "All right, I'm good," she said.

He smiled as he continued on to SFIT. Hiro felt good about it. He knew this was where he belonged and where Tadashi would want him to be.

At the robotics lab, Hiro unpacked one last box that he had brought from his garage lab at home. He took out Baymax's rocket fist and set it down on his desk. He gave the fist a little fist bump and it opened slightly. Hiro spotted a glint of something inside. He peeled open the fingers and found—Baymax's health-care chip!

Hiro could barely contain his excitement. He knew just what to do.

After working late at the lab for several nights, it was finally ready. Hiro held his breath. Then he let out a big "OW!"

The red suitcase opened and the soft, familiar shape Hiro had come to love inflated in front of him. Hiro shouted with joy as the robot voice he'd missed so much said, "Hello, Hiro. I am Baymax, your personal health-care companion."

ビッグ・ヒーロー6

On a wind turbine overlooking San Fransokyo Bay, six friends who happened to be superheroes looked down on the city they were committed to protect.

"We didn't set out to be superheroes. But sometimes life doesn't go the way you planned," Hiro said. "The good thing is my brother wanted to help a lot of people, and that's what we're going to do. Who are we?"

The answer was clear, and they said it together: "Big Hero Six!"